To our good Blaydock friends. and in Vintage but no murders.
Good luck on your first

Mystery at a Country Inn

trip to America and the Colonies.

CW01604519

Mystery at a Country Inn

Philip Owen

Berkshire Traveller Press
STOCKBRIDGE, MASSACHUSETTS

SELECTED TITLES FROM THE BERKSHIRE TRAVELLER PRESS

Country Inns and Back Roads, North America
Country Inns and Back Roads, Europe
Country Inn Cookbook
A Spy at Ticonderoga

Copyright © 1979 by Judson Philips

All rights reserved

No part of this book may be reproduced in any form without written permission from the publisher.

10 9 8 7 6 5 4 3 2 1

Cover by Jan Lindstrom

Library of Congress #79-52082
ISBN 0-912944-54-4
Printed by Studley Press, Dalton, Massachusetts U.S.A.

Part One

One

It was just before one in the morning when the Duchess, occupying the corner suite on the second floor of the Red Cardinal Inn, unable to sleep, looked out the window at the full moon that was moving around to her side of the building. The moon was instantly reflected in the swimming pool that was just below the lady's window.

At first, as she told it later, she thought what she saw was some kind of bizarre mirroring. A man appeared to be lying on the bottom of the pool looking up at her, his mouth twisted in a kind of sardonic grin. She leaned out the window, she reported, trying to locate where the man really was. Then she realized that where he really was was at the bottom of the pool. No illusion. It was for real, and he had to be dead because he hadn't moved for minutes.

The Duchess screamed at the top of her lungs. For a ninety-four-year-old woman she managed a blood curdling sound.

You've heard it on television commercials for the state lottery. "What would you do if you suddenly found you'd won a half a million dollars?" And people answer: "Pay off the mortgage—faint—build a house for my parents—travel—" and like that. Well, I had come into a half million dollars, quite legally, but with a string attached to it. The string tied me to Miss Martha Walton, known to the staff at the Red Cardinal Inn as "The Duchess." I was entitled to the money if I would watch out for Miss Walton, care for her, see to it that she lived out her life where she wanted and how she wanted.

The lady was eighty-nine-years-old when she became my responsibility. I didn't think the job would last long. When the old girl passed peacefully on I would be rich without strings attached. But on the night the Duchess saw a dead man in the Red Cardinal's pool I had been waiting for that peaceful passing for five years. It wasn't an unpleasant job, you understand. It simply didn't involve any action, and up to the moment I inherited the Duchess, my life had been all action. Incidentally, I was thirty-nine-years old the night the Duchess screamed.

I started out my adult life as a cop. I guess I was what the good guys call a bad cop. I was too quick to use my legal weapon, too quick to move in on some criminal punk before I read him his rights. I was finally suspended from the force for shooting a guy between the eyes who drew a gun on me. He turned out to be an off-duty cop who thought I had just robbed a super-market. Actually I was chasing the guy who had robbed the market and I thought this guy drawing a gun was an accomplice. Bad luck for him—and for me, as far as my career as a cop was concerned.

There was a lot in the papers and on the tube about it. It looked as if I was going to have a hell of a time getting any kind of a job anywhere. "The mad-dog killer cop," one of the tabloids called me. I thought that label would fix my wagon for keeps, but it turned out to be a passport to my kind of action and, eventually, a half-a-million bucks.

Wilfred Krider sent someone to find me when that "mad-dog killer cop" story broke. There has been a lot written about Wilfred Krider; there is a best-selling biography of him out now called *Blood and Power.* I could have told the author a lot more about the bloody side of Wilfred Krider's life than he was able to research. I was twenty-four-years old when, a discredited cop, I went to work for Krider as his personal bodyguard and private strong-arm operator. He was a vigorous eighty-four when he dropped dead jogging along a quiet back road on his estate in the Connecticut town of Camden. Camden is the town where the Red Cardinal Inn is located, and where the Duchess looked out her window and saw a dead man in the swimming pool.

I worked for Wilfred Krider, not Krider Industries, of which he was the founder, the President for years, and the Chairman of the Board the day his heart stopped. I have to tell you the Old Man never thought he would die of natural causes. I can still see the look of surprise on his dead face when I picked him up off that dusty road in Camden. Krider Industries owns half the world, oil, steel, airlines, newspapers and TV stations, hotels, invaluable real estate, copper—you name it. Their holdings blanket the world. In addition to the United States they sit on money and power in the Middle East, the Far East, Africa, Europe, South America. Wilfred Krider was the master puppeteer who maneuvered the lives, deaths, and fortunes of thousands of people. There wasn't a day that some fanatic didn't want to eliminate him. In the last ten years of his life nobody even came close because Dan Burton, "the mad-dog killer cop," was hired to protect him. I have to say, without vanity, that I did the job.

Krider told me about his will a year or so before he died. I couldn't be as close to him as I was and not know some intimate facts about him. He was married, with a son, two daughters, and a raft of grandchildren. But his private life, his personal emotions, were centered around the woman who had been his mistress for forty-five years. That woman was, of course, Miss Martha Walton, the Duchess.

They met in their middle lives; he was four years younger than she. She had been a glamorous show girl, nightclub performer and musical comedy star. He was the king of an empire. He kept her in Paris, in London, on the Riviera, in Rome, in Cairo. Wherever he went, surrounded by family and business associates, she was close by, ready for him whenever he wanted her. It wasn't just a sex union. It was a great love story that somebody ought to write. He went to her with his problems, his headaches, his fears, his joys. Don't ask me why Wilfred didn't divorce his wife. Perhaps fifty years ago it was unthinkable, and later he had developed a pattern that was too good, too satisfactory to risk changing.

The day Krider told me about his will is not one I'm likely to forget. He had bought a huge estate in the Connecticut town of Camden, and in those last years he operated from there. I lived in the big house with him, never out of reach, out of sight. Danger followed him wherever he was. In the village, a couple of miles away, was the Red Cardinal Inn. Miss Martha Walton was established there in a two-room suite on the second floor. How they met, where they met, how they spent the time they had together, is a secret I don't choose to reveal while the old girl is still alive. But the day of the will Krider told me he was leaving the Duchess a million dollars in cold cash, and me a half million for keeping him alive and being a loyal friend, provided—provided I would look out for the Duchess as long as she lived.

And then, one day when he was jogging, he dropped dead. A great man, a great villain, a tender, faithful lover.

How he would know whether or not I looked out for the Duchess I couldn't say, but he had been so all-powerful in his lifetime I took it for granted I'd be struck by lightning if I failed him. So I rented a cottage across the street from the inn, bought some clothes the Old Man might not have approved of and a bright yellow Volkswagen I *knew* he wouldn't approve of. I began spending money on old record albums—being close to the Duchess had aroused my interest in old Broadway musicals and some of the great musical comedy stars and singers of the past. Now, I was able to become a collector in earnest. Before long I was a real music buff—knew almost as much about that world as the Duchess.

Then came that hot night in August when I was listening to and looking at Laura Stark as she played the piano. She was the summer entertainment in the lounge at the Red Cardinal. Laura had the kind of a face I'd like to become accustomed to, and if her glances in my direction were any indication, she was reading my mind. Then, my happy reverie was abruptly broken when the Duchess screamed.

I saw Mr. Chips, the bartender, vault over the mahogany bar and run out through the french doors onto the flagstone terrace that separated the inn from the pool. There were just five customers in the lounge at the time, plus Chips and Laura Stark,the girl at the piano. There was me, and two young guys who were staying at the inn while they competed in a golf tournament at the Camden Country Club, and a middle-aged couple named Townsend who were just spending the night on their way to Vermont, or Canada, or some place.

Laura Stark was a lovely young thing, about twenty, twenty-one years old, who played show tunes and old jazz that she was much too young to have heard when they originated. She had an enormous repertory and all you had to do was ask and she'd play that tune you danced to when you were in college, or you'd heard on the radio when you were making love to some special dame. She knew a lot of the lyrics, too, and sang them in a kind of Lee Wiley manner, if you remember that extraordinary chanteuse. She stopped in the middle of one of my favorites—"It Was Just One Of Those Things"—when the Duchess's screaming split the New England night. She grabbed hold of my arm, her fingers cold as ice, and her eyes wide with fear.

We all followed Chips out onto the terrace. The Duchess, like an aged prisoner in a tower in some Gothic novel, was at her window, pointing down at the pool. Then she was gone.

I looked down into the pool and saw the man, leering up at the moon. I saw him, and, after a fashion, I knew him.

About ten years ago I had shot him twice, once in the leg when he tried to run, once in the arm when he'd reached for his own gun. The gent on the bottom of the pool had been after Wilfred Krider on that occasion. He didn't make it past me, but he got away after I'd wounded him. I'd gone to cover the Old Man. When other help on the Krider estate went to look for the would-be assassin he had crawled away. There were tire marks and footprints which told the story of an accomplice. He couldn't have made it alone. How do I know? When I shoot a man in the knee cap he doesn't walk away.

The two young golfers brushed past me and went into the pool after the man. It was the shallow end, not more than three feet deep. They pulled him out, tried pumping water out of his lungs. One of them tried mouth-to-mouth resuscitation. It was all quite pointless. I saw the hole just at the edge of his hairline by his left ear where a bullet had been fired into his brain. This time my hit-man wasn't going anywhere.

A violent murder in the town of Camden, on the grounds of the gracious old Red Cardinal Inn, was as unlikely as finding a spider in your strawberry mousse at a gourmet banquet.

Ten years ago the Krider estate up Camden Mountain, surrounded by a high, electrified fence, populated by a small army of guards, had been another story. But the Old Man was dead, the fence was gone, the guards were gone. Maxwell Krider, his son, lived there, peacefully rich, with his wife and his son Joshua, who was a rather objectionable lush, visited by grandchildren and nieces and nephews. The blood-and-guts days of Wilfred Krider were history. Maxwell Krider had nothing to do with Krider Industries except to collect his stock dividends. He had never had the stomach, or the taste, or the skills for managing the empire his father had built. Camden Mountain was peaceful these days.

As for the town of Camden, it was a place for retired, wealthy people. There are two or three private schools in the area where rich men send their sons—and, these days, their daughters. There are ski resorts north of the town, there is in a neighboring town, a race track where automobile freaks congregate for races three or four times a year. The Red Cardinal Inn draws customers from all these sources, and from the "leaf peepers" who travel through New England in the fall to enjoy the changing colors. It is peaceful, unhurried, uncluttered.

The Red Cardinal Inn is a place for gracious hospitality. It sprawls over a piece of ground in the center of the village, the scarlet bird for which it is named painted on its welcoming sign. The original inn, added to over the years, dates back to before the American Revolution. The walls are panelled in aged oak and pine, there are big stone fireplaces in all the public rooms. The food is excellent, the wine cellar exceptional, the innkeepers, Richard and Ruth Carson, are experts at the art of making their guests feel welcome and wanting to return. A murder at the Red Cardinal was unthinkable, and yet a man lay on the pool terrace with a hole in his head and the scars of other wounds on one knee cap and one forearm.

Chips, the bartender, had gone back inside to phone the state police. The rest of us stood huddled around the dead man. It was a warm summer night, but somehow the night air had taken on a chill. Laura Stark was still hanging onto my arm; there was something about her that brought out all my protective instincts. I patted her trembling fingers reassuringly. I looked up at the corner room. I ought to make sure the Duchess was okay, but I didn't.

"Any I.D. on him?" I asked one of the golfers who had tried to breathe air into dead lungs and was still kneeling beside the body.

My hit-man was dressed in tan summer slacks, a checked

sports shirt, and open-toed sandals without socks; ordinary, informal summer wear. The golfer went through his pockets. There was no wallet.

"Twenty-odd bucks in bills and change," the golfer said. "No car keys."

In the country it's unusual for a man to be without car keys. You can't get anywhere without a car. If he had a car and left the keys in it there should be a driver's license and a registration.

"Any of you ever see him before?" the golfer asked.

Laura, and the Townsends, and the other golfer all said they hadn't. I kept what I knew to myself for the moment. I'd seen him before, but I had no idea who he was, only what he was.

"Somebody better check on Miss Walton," Laura said. "Probably scared out of her wits."

I knew better than that. The Duchess didn't scare easily.

What a woman! Would you believe that a tough bastard like me, fifty-five years her junior, could be just a little bit in love with that old broad? She must have been something when Wilfred Krider caught up with her, tall, long-legged, red-haired, with high cheekbones, eyes that twinkle with humor, a wide, generous mouth, an overall, inate elegance. She can swear like a sailor, loves a risqué joke, but can be the great lady if she chooses. She still walks tall and straight. I have watched her cross the lobby of the Red Cardinal like a nineteenth-century man-o'-war under full sail. You get out of her way if you don't want to be run down. She wears makeup, but it's expertly applied. She must dye her hair but it looks for real. She doesn't look like an old woman trying to look young, but an old woman trying to look beautiful, and, by God, making it. She dresses expensively, but in the period when she and Wilfred Krider got together—the 1920s. Her clothes look lovely on her. "When I buy clothes," she once told me, "I'm like Alice, going down the rabbit hole, to the end of World War I, when Will Krider and I first met and fell in love. That's when I want to live my life. I dress for those days and not today's vulgarities."

I remember wondering where she could get clothes from that period except in someone's attic or at a rummage sale, and yet her clothes looked spotlessly fresh and new. I found out that a young woman of seventy-seven, who had been designing and making Martha Walton's clothes for fifty years was still running them up on her little Singer sewing machine.

The Duchess has a unique place in the life at the Red Cardinal. She is the inn's only permanent guest. It is the result of another protection set up around Martha Walton by the man who loved her so dearly. When Wilfred retired with his family to run the Krider empire from Camden Mountain he bought the Red Cardinal Inn from the then-owner. That was twenty years ago. It was a place for Martha to live close by him. If he owned it he could be sure of the treatment, the service she would get. He hired Dick and Ruth Carson to run the place for him. Dick was something of a genius at the business of innkeeping. Not only was there a constant flow of transient guests, many of them repeaters, but it became a kind of social center for the residents of the area. People from Camden and the surrounding towns dined there, gave private parties there, congregated in the lounge in the evenings where they were bound to meet congenial friends. Dick made a substantial profit for the owner, who didn't care about profits, but only about the comfort and security of the lady he loved. Dick and Ruth Carson both made the Duchess feel wanted, made her feel that the Red Cardinal was her home, socialized with her when she felt like company. The Duchess must have given them very high marks, because after a couple of years Wilfred Krider sold the inn to Dick and Ruth—rumor has it for a dollar—with the understanding that the deed to the property wouldn't be registered in their name until the Duchess came to the end of her road. Dick, like me, had everything he could have asked for in return for his services to Wilfred, provided the Duchess didn't communicate with Wilfred in the Great

Beyond and ask him to drop a thunderbolt on us. Dick and I shared something else. It was no onerous duty for us to look out for the lady. It was a pleasure. It even had its business advantages for Dick. The Duchess became a sort of Red Cardinal landmark. Returning guests looked for her at her table in the dining room, or in the booth in the lounge where she held court two or three nights a week. Some of them were privileged to get to know her, to stop by her table to exchange quips. She was an original, one of a kind, memorable. Someday she would be missing, and travelers would be sad when they heard it.

I didn't get to check on the lady right away because Chips came out from the lounge accompanied by a state trooper. The barracks had contacted a patrol car that was cruising in the Camden area. I knew Sergeant Lacey in a casual way. He is a type; blond, with cold eyes, who looks at you like you'd just run over a five-year-old child instead of driving fifty miles an hour in a forty-five-mile zone when he says, "May I see your license, please."

We all backed away from the body as he knelt beside it. He gave Chips that cold look. "You didn't tell me it was a homicide," he said.

"I didn't know," Chips said. "I thought he drowned." Chips is a story in himself, to be told later. He is tall, stoop-shouldered, with thinning sandy hair, wearing shell-rimmed glasses that give him an owlish look. He looks more like a schoolteacher than a bartender. The fact is, he once was a schoolteacher and he isn't a bartender. He was closing the bar that night because the regular man had had to leave early.

"Shot in front of the left ear," Lacey said. "Call the barracks and tell them we've got a homicide." Chips took off. "Who is he?"

None of us knew.

"Ever see him before?"

The others hadn't.

"I did, ten years ago," I said. "He came to Camden

Mountain gunning for Wilfred Krider. I winged him twice but he got away while I was trying to get the old man under cover. You'll find a record of the whole thing in your files at the barracks."

"His name?"

"I have no idea. He got away clean at the time, with help from someone."

"You haven't seen him since then?"

"If I had he'd be in jail, not here."

"You haven't seen him hanging around the Inn here or in the town?"

"No."

"Who found him?"

"We were all in the lounge when the old lady up in that corner started screaming," the first-aid golfer said. "We ran out here and she was pointing down at the pool. Greg and I went in and dragged him out."

"Your name?"

"Bob Spencer. Greg Wallace and I are playing here in a golf tournament at the Camden Country Club."

"Your names?" Lacey asked the middle-aged couple, who didn't look at all happy about the way their evening had turned out.

"I'm Arthur Townsend," the man said. "This is my wife, Caroline. Summit, New Jersey. We're just driving north at the start of a vacation. We were in the lounge, listening to this young lady at the piano, when the woman upstairs started to scream."

Lacey knew who Laura and I were. "Hi, Laura," he said, sounding human for the first time. His smile was obviously meant for her alone, I noticed. Laura didn't say anything, her fingers tightening on my wrist.

"You don't mention hearing the shot," Lacey said.

None of us had heard it.

"You'd better get the old lady down here," Lacey said. "The homicide boys will want to talk to her."

That was my cue. I reached out and gave Laura's arm a little squeeze. "Sit tight, doll," I said. "I'll be back."

Chips followed me into the inn. Chips is someone I think of as a good friend. He is as much of a landmark at the Red Cardinal as the Duchess. Returning guests ask for him, just to find out how he is. He is Mr. Everything at the inn. Dick Carson once told me how he came to hire Chips.

"It was when old man Krider first engaged me to run the inn," Dick told me. "I was putting together a new staff, and I was complaining one night to someone about the problem of finding a mop man, a clean-up man. There's no profit in a mop-man. He'll steal your beer and drink your liquor. Whoever I was talking to asked why I didn't hire a cured alcoholic?" Dick laughed as he remembered it. "It sounded like an idiotic idea, but the next morning I called someone who was in Alcoholics Anonymous and a couple of hours later Chips showed up. He was a schoolteacher who had gotten in trouble with booze, been fired, gone down to the bottom of the hill, was willing to work at anything, and he told me frankly that he was taking it one day at a time. There was something in his quiet confidence that made me want to take a chance on him. I have to tell you I don't know of his ever taking a drink in the twenty years he's worked for me. He handles it, serves it, buys it for me, but never touches it."

"He does a hell of a lot more than mop floors these days," I said.

"Funny thing," Dick says, "But I'd have to look in the records to tell you what his real name is. When people found out he'd been a schoolteacher someone dubbed him 'Mr. Chips' and it's stuck. He insists on being paid in cash, so I never write a check for him. Like you say, he does everything. Oh, he mops, cleans up the men's room, goes for the mail, orders supplies, has talked a couple of would-be suicides from jumping off the water tower, handles out-of-order drunks like a magician, mends machinery. Best of all he's become a friend I'd trust with my life. That's Chips for you."

I don't much like cooking for myself, and I don't want to have someone come in to get breakfast for me. Not infrequently someone has shared my bed with me who wouldn't like to have the news broadcast at the Camden post office. So I breakfast every morning at the inn, which is just across the street from my cottage. The first person I see, every day, is Chips, tidying up the lobby, or sweeping the front porch, or shoveling snow in winter. We pass the time of day with brilliant conversation, like "Is it hot enough for you—or cold enough—or wet enough." If I didn't appear for breakfast I think Chips would have come across the street to check on me. I know damn well if I didn't see him about I'd have gone straight to the desk to make inquiries. In this unimportant way we were part of each other's routine. He was a favorite of the Duchess's which was another link between us. More than once I've helped Chips escort some over-active customer out of the lounge. I enjoyed the exercise. We made jokes about some of the inn's eccentric guests.

I learned a lot about country inns and what makes them tick in my conversations with Chips.

"Each one is different," Chips told me, "which sets them apart from chain-hotels and the modern motels. Each one of them expresses the tastes and aspirations of the individual innkeepers. The Red Cardinal speaks for Dick and Ruth Carson—and their kids. The Quigley sisters who run the gift shop are Ruth's aunts. Strong family business, key to the success of this kind of operation."

That morning it must have been rough for Dick Carson. His wife Ruth, on whom he depended for endless details, had gone off to the Midwest somewhere to be with her mother who was seriously ill. His two kids, just out of college, had been given the summer off to visit and explore other country inns across the country. Dick was having to face this crisis without help he normally depended on heavily.

"You say your encounter with this guy was ten years ago?" Chips asked, when we were inside the inn together.

"That's right," I said.

"I remember," Chips said. "A police artist drew a picture of him from your description. Not far off. He wears his hair longer now. Funny, I can't remember if it was just the picture or if I saw him myself somewhere, sometime. You never knew why he was gunning for Wilfred Krider?"

"There were so many people in so many parts of the world who wanted Krider's head on a platter there was no way to guess which one of them had hired a hit-man to do him in."

"But he had an accomplice who got him away?"

"Had to be. He wasn't walking after I'd finished with him."

"No description of the accomplice?"

"I never saw him, didn't know he existed at the moment." I said. "I brought the hit-man down, shot him in the arm when he reached for a gun. I left him lying there and went to make sure the Old Man was okay. I passed the word, and some of the other guards went to pick up the killer. He was gone."

"It must have been the police drawing," Chips said. "I could have sworn I'd seen him before when I first looked at him there in the pool. You suppose he was interested in the Kriders again?"

"If he was, they sure represented bad luck for him," I said.

"He wasn't traveling alone that first time," Chips said. "I wonder if there was someone with him this time?"

"No way to guess," I said.

Chips gave me a perplexed look. "Not a pleasant thought, but we've got a killer crawling around somewhere in the woodwork."

It's strange how your mind works in a crisis. I had been trained as a cop, as a detective. There were a lot of questions to be asked and answered. Sooner or later the proper wheels would start turning in my head, but right now my job was to check out the Duchess.

Not many people got to visit with the Duchess in her second-floor suite. The floor maid knew it, Chips knew it, I knew it, Dick and Ruth Carson knew it. It was a madhouse. If a stranger walked in he would have been bewildered by the disorder. The sitting room was large, with four windows looking out on the swimming pool, but it was so cluttered that it seemed small. There was a built-in bookcase against one wall, but there were almost no books in it. It was filled with Staffordshire dogs, dolls, toy animals out of a Winnie-the-Pooh collection, carved ivory elephants. On the opposite wall were framed photographs of famous leading men of fifty years ago—John Barrymore as *Hamlet,* Roland Young as General Burgoyne in *The Devil's Disciple,* Leslie Howard, and God knows how many others, all autographed affectionately to Martha Walton. All men.

"Old friends," was all she ever said about them.

I suspect most of the young Lotharios of the day were after Martha Walton, probably some of them made it before she fell forever into the arms of Wilfred Krider.

If you wanted to look at the pictures closely you'd have had to pick your way through stacks of newspapers and old magazines on the floor, in chairs, against the walls. The Collier brothers would have been envious if they could have seen it. Yet I suspect that if you'd asked the Duchess for the Op-ed page of the *New York Times* for a certain day twenty-five years ago she could have picked it out for you without hesitation. Disorder to you, complete orderliness to her.

She opened the door the moment I knocked, tall, her dyed red hair in perfect order, her makeup artistically applied.

"Thank God, you've come," she said.

"You shaken up?" I asked her.

"Like hell," she said. "I can't get this goddam dress hooked up." She has a husky voice that hasn't been helped by seventy-five years of cigarette smoking and brandy sipping.

She turned her back to me. The black taffeta dress had to be fastened at the back with little hook-and-eye gadgets that I couldn't see, only feel for in the dim light.

"You ought to have a zipper on this, luv," I said.

"Damn things make you look like a brief case," she said. "I must say Chips is a lot cleverer at this than you are, Daniel."

"Mr. Everything," I said.

"A very dear person," she said. "Do hurry, Daniel."

"Doing my best, dear," I said. "But what's the hurry?"

"The police, obviously, will want to talk to me. Did you expect me to appear in my nightgown?"

I got the kinky hooks hooked, and she took off into the bedroom—which I'd never seen. She uses a perfume like nothing I've ever smelled before; delicate, seductive, suggesting a young, very glamorous woman. I commented on it to her once, and she told me Wilfred had had it specially concocted for her in Paris. "No reason why an old woman should smell of camphor and mothballs," she said.

She came out of the bedroom, slipping some heavy bracelets studded with emeralds on her wrists. She had draped an emerald pendant around her neck. She loved jewelry. Wilfred Krider could have bought her the art treasures of the world, but jewelry seems to have been all she cared for. She must have had a small fortune in gems.

"Shall we go down?" she said.

Ninety-four! You would expect her to totter a little, to lean heavily on my arm, to grip the stair rail. Not the Duchess. She took the stairway down under a full head of steam. I'd learned some secrets about her over my years of guardianship. She prepared for movement. I've been sitting with her in the Red Cardinal's bar and suggested that we go into the dining room for dinner.

"In a minute or two, Daniel," she'd say. I realized she was gathering her energy, her resources of strength, for a moment of action. "Now!" she would say, and take off.

That early morning she made an entrance into the lounge. Chips was behind the stick again. The bar was legally closed, but Dick Carson was serving everybody on the house. He had arrived, looking like a man who'd been asleep and hastily put on yesterday's clothes when someone woke him. He has one of a half-dozen small cottages on the inn grounds. The golfers were there, and the Townsend couple, and Laura Stark, and Captain Ed Folwell of the state police, their homicide man. Folwell and I had had dealings years ago over the vanishing hit-man who now lay dead out on the terrace. He is a chunky, grey-haired man with a weathered face and very bright blue eyes that make you think he could read the label on the inside of your shirt collar when he looks at you. A good cop, in my judgment. Lacey and other troopers were, I gathered, out on the terrace with the body.

The Duchess cruised up to the bar. "The President's Room is hardly the place to hold a wake," she said. "I'll have a brandy, Chips."

In 1904 Teddy Roosevelt had stopped at the Red Cardinal for lunch, and the then-owner had named the taproom "The President's Room." I looked up the history of the inn one day in the local library and found out that John Adams had spent a night there on his way from Boston to Washington, and that Cal Coolidge had spent a weekend there in the 1920s, fishing in the lake with the Indian name. The Duchess is the only person who still insists on calling the lounge the President's Room. She likes the past a hell of a lot more than she likes the present. Incidentally, the Camden library is now called The Wilfred Krider Memorial Library, and there is a wing in the hospital in the next town named after him, and an art gallery and theater out on Route 12. Like a lot of tough originals who got rich cutting assorted throats, Wilfred Krider had been most generous to the community he'd adopted. Camden owed him more than his plot in the local cemetery.

Ed Folwell, the trooper captain, approached the Duchess as she sipped the brandy Chips had poured her. She'd produced a cigarette from her jeweled handbag and Folwell held his lighter for her.

"You remember me, Miss Walton?" he asked.

"Of course. You're Lieutenant Folwell," she said.

"It's Captain now, Miss Walton," he said. "Burton tell

you the dead man is the Mr. X we were all interested in ten years ago?"

"He did not," she said, and gave me a dirty look.

"Getting you hooked up it slipped my mind," I said.

"It doesn't matter," she said, "because I know who he is."

That got her center stage. She turned to Chips.

"What's his name, Chips? He's the television repair man you sent to my rooms day before yesterday."

"I didn't send any repair man to your room, Miss Walton," Chips said. "I didn't know there was anything wrong with your TV. If I had I'd have fixed it for you myself."

"Nonsense," she said. "I came back from my morning walk with Teddy, and he was there, working on the set. I took it for granted you sent him. Or you, Dick?"

"I didn't, Martha," Dick Carson said. He's the only person I know who calls her by her first name. "I've just looked at him. He isn't local, not anyone I've ever seen before."

Bear in mind that over the years thousands of people pass through the Red Cardinal, transients, locals. Part of the business of running an inn is remembering faces and names. If Dick had never seen him before, then he had almost certainly never been in the Red Cardinal.

"What was wrong with your set?" Dick asked.

"I didn't realize there was anything wrong with it," the Duchess said. "Something about a condenser, he said. He refused a tip when I offered it to him. One of your nice young people, I thought, Richard."

I guess anyone under sixty-five is young to the Duchess. The dead man was no kid.

"You saw him in the pool and screamed?" Folwell asked her. "Was it the sound of a shot that called your attention to him?"

"It was the full moon," the Duchess said. "At my age, Lieutenant, you don't let a full moon go by, even if you have to look at it alone."

Folwell was never going to get his new rank. He had been

"Lieutenant" to her ten years ago and he was going to stay "Lieutenant."

"Let's see," he said. "You were up in the corner rooms. You went to the window to look at the full moon and you saw this man lying in the bottom of the pool?"

"And let out the loudest yell I could muster," the Duchess said.

"You must have been twenty, thirty feet away from him. Moonlight. Under water. Not too clear, I should think. You thought he looked like this TV repair man?"

"I did not say he *looked* like the TV man," the Duchess said. "I said he *was* the TV man."

"I wonder if you'd mind taking a close look at him," Folwell asked. "Just to be sure."

"Why should I mind?" She finished her brandy and started toward the french doors. She stopped by Laura Stark, who had grabbed hold of my arm again. "When you get to be my age, child, which God forbid," the Duchess said, "you'll know that murder is not an uncommon happening. Unless the dead man is someone close to you there's no reason for your knees to be knocking together."

She went out onto the terrace, followed by Folwell.

Two

When a man is trying to draw a gun on you to kill you, what he looks like gets etched in your memory rather permanently. I was the only person who had seen the hit-man when he came after Wilfred Krider. I had caught him trying to slip through a window into the old man's study. He ran, but I brought him down with a shot in the knee. He rolled over on the lawn outside the window and for a moment we stared at each other. He wouldn't ever forget me, either. Then he reached for his gun and I shot him in the arm. That makes it sound as though I was Buffalo Bill or some famous gunslinger, but I'd always scored very high on the police range when I was a cop. I left him there, writhing in the grass. I had to find Krider. There was a chance the hit-man had been on his way out and not on his way in. I ran into one of the housemen who'd heard the shots and told him he'd find the wounded man outside. I found Krider having his lunch on the terrace, oblivious to what had happened.

The houseman had gotten help and gone out to take the hit-man, but he was gone. There was never any description of him except the one I gave to Folwell at the time. The police artist did a damn good job of a likeness, and though it was circulated all over the East and to the FBI in Washington, and the CIA, no one ever bit on it.

He was back now, back and dead. Not a shadow of a

doubt about it. The Duchess was just as certain that he was the TV repair man she'd found in her rooms two days ago. Since she hadn't complained about her set, and since no one had sent for anyone to look at it, our man had obviously been faking when she found him in her rooms. Why had he been there? None of us could overlook the coincidence that on the dead man's first visit he had been after Wilfred Krider. Ten years later he is posing as a TV repair man in the rooms where Wilfred Krider's mistress lived. There had to be a connection of some sort.

The Duchess wasn't able to suggest what it might be. Folwell brought her back from the terrace. I thought she looked a little green around the gills, in spite of her somewhat hard-boiled advice to Laura. The dead man wasn't pretty to look at. But, she insisted, he was the man she had found in her rooms two days ago claiming to be there to repair her TV set.

"You had no conversation with him?" Captain Folwell asked her.

"I was surprised to find him there," she said. "He said he was just finishing with the set. The set wasn't mine, you understand. It comes with the room. I hadn't complained about it, but I supposed Richard or Chips had decided to have it checked out. I went into the bedroom to freshen up, and when I came out he was just leaving. He said the set was fixed, I offered him a tip, he refused it. 'It's a pleasure to be of service to you, Miss Walton,' he said. That was the extent of our conversation. I didn't expect him to become a part of my social life."

"Was he carrying tools?"

"I suppose he must have been. I really didn't notice."

Folwell glanced at his wrist watch. "It's 2 a.m. on Thursday, Miss Walton. You say two days ago. Are you thinking of this as Wednesday night? Was it Tuesday or Monday that you found him in your room?"

"You're right, of course," she said, without hesitation. "It was Monday."

"You said you'd been on your morning walk with 'Teddy.' May I ask who Teddy is?"

She gave him a rasping little laugh. "You'll think I'm a dotty old woman," she said. "Teddy is a teddy bear. He was given to me many years ago as a good luck charm. I take him with me most places I go, which is almost nowhere. My morning and evening walks, sometimes to the dining room and here in the lounge when I need company. I didn't bring him with me now because I knew there'd be a lot of strangers. Teddy doesn't like strangers." She gave Folwell a bland smile.

I could see that Folwell decided he was dealing with senility. Teddy was no stranger to those of us who centered our lives around the Red Cardinal. I knew his story. Wilfred Krider had given him to the Duchess before the opening of a Broadway musical in which she had been appearing. The play was a smash hit and Teddy's good luck magic was established. Then she turned herself lock, stock, and barrel over to Krider, and that, she considered, was great good fortune. Teddy had traveled around the world with her, to all of the places to which she followed Krider. I was told that F.A.O. Schwarz, the fabulous New York toy store, had recovered him once and replaced his little shoe-button eyes. I think the Duchess would have worn him around her slender neck if he'd been a little less bulky.

Folwell tried again. "There is no doubt in Dan Burton's mind, or mine, that the dead man is the assassin who tried to kill Wilfred Krider ten years ago."

She looked at me. "Will was very grateful to you on that occasion, Daniel. I think that may be why you inherited me."

"It's no secret, Miss Walton, that you and Mr. Krider were—very close friends."

"Quite a bit more than that, Lieutenant," she said.

"So this man who tried to kill Wilfred Krider found his way to your rooms. Can you guess why? Because it wasn't to fix your TV set."

"I haven't the remotest idea," she said. "If, as you all say, he wasn't a TV man, then perhaps he was just a common sneak thief."

"Are you missing anything?"

"Not that I know of."

"You keep a lot of jewelry up there, Martha," Dick Carson said. "Have you checked it out lately? Since Monday morning?"

"No, I had no reason to. But I can tell you no amount of it was taken. Maybe a single piece. Take me ten minutes to check it."

"I wish you would, Miss Walton."

I watched her, knowing that she was gathering herself together. And then she took off, boldly, briskly. Folwell watched her go.

"She's a little off her rocker, no?" he said.

"No," I said.

Dick Carson laughed. "Don't be fooled by Teddy, Ed. I'll bet you carry a Kennedy half-dollar around in your pocket—or something. Mine is an Indian head penny I've got fastened to my key ring."

We never did find out if Folwell carried anything for good luck, because Sergeant Lacey and Dr. Chance, the medical examiner, came in from the terrace. Chance, a grey-haired little man with a scraggly grey mustache, dropped a bomb on us.

"You got a problem, Captain," he said. "Your friend out there on the terrace has been dead for quite a while. Rigor pretty well advanced. I can only make an educated guess until I do an autopsy, but I'd say two or three days."

"He was alive Monday morning at nine-thirty," Folwell said.

"He got his comeuppance not long after that," the doctor said.

Folwell shook his head. "Somebody hid the body or has been lugging it around for two days and then dropped it off in the pool this morning!"

"He was long dead when he went in the pool," Dr. Chance said. "Some contusions on the rib cage and the legs made after death. I'll try to give you a closer guess when I've carved him up, but I'm not far off."

"Crazy business," Folwell said.

"See you around," Dr. Chance said. "I suppose it's okay to move him?"

"That seems to be a way of life—or death—for him," Folwell said. "Moving around! He's all yours, Doctor."

I knew, without his saying so, that Folwell's whole game plan had to be changed. There were fifty-six transient guests in the Red Cardinal that night, plus the Duchess, plus the night staff and the day staff coming on in a few hours. He had intended to insist that all of them take a look at the dead man, who had presumably been shot not long before he was found. If he had been dead since Monday, most of the transients hadn't been here then.

"When could somebody have taken the risk of dumping a dead man in the pool?" he asked.

"It would have to have been after midnight," Chips said. "It was a warm night. People were swimming out there till ten or eleven, and others took their drinks out onto the terrace. It was a lovely moonlit night. It was just a little before twelve-thirty when the customers thinned out. Dan, and the two golfers, and Mr. and Mrs. Townsend were left, listening to Laura's piano. It was about one when the Duchess started screaming. So you'd have to guess between twelve-thirty and one."

"How can you figure it?" Folwell asked. He was simmering. "There are windows, lots of 'em, overlooking the pool. There are people in here only a few yards away. It's a full moon, almost like daylight. Somebody lugs a dead body right out in the open and dumps it in the pool! Only a lunatic would risk something like that."

"So we're dealing with a lunatic," I said.

"Are there places around here you could hide a body for a

couple of days?" Folwell asked. "Guests, maids, in and out of all the bedrooms. Public rooms in constant use. Your kitchens, storerooms, freezers, furnaces—all in the basement, with dozens of the help moving around all the time."

"Let's not decide the body was hidden here," Dick Carson said. He was already listening to the radio and TV shows that would come on the air in a while, none of them good advertising for the Red Cardinal. "Somebody could have been carrying the body around in the trunk of a car for a couple of days."

"So why does he risk bringing it here and dumping it in your pool? It's as though he had a reason for wanting it found here. If he just wanted to be rid of it, there are thousands of acres of countryside where he could have dumped it and it would never have been found." Folwell drew a deep breath. "Riddles, yet," he said.

He was a thorough man, and I could see what was coming. Every inch of the Red Cardinal would be searched. The trunks of automobiles that had been here since Monday, which would include all the day and night staffs, would be examined. And somewhere, there was a faceless person who had killed a man and disposed of him in this bizarre fashion.

"There are a couple of things you could do if you feel like helping," Folwell said to me.

"Sure."

"Check out with Miss Walton and see if our dead friend ripped her off."

"Easy."

"Ten years ago we didn't get to talk to her," Folwell said. "The whole damn town knew that she was Will Krider's girl friend, but we didn't question her at the time because we knew she wouldn't tell us anything that Krider wouldn't tell us. But maybe he talked to her in private. Maybe she knows something about who was after him that she'd be willing to tell us, now that her man isn't in danger anymore."

"I can try," I said.

"And the Kriders up the mountain," Folwell said. "There's no way of guessing what this is all about, but they may have been threatened, may know something about our man."

"I don't win any popularity contests with Maxwell Krider and his family," I said. "I got a chunk of money from the old man they may wish they had. They also like to pretend that Martha Walton doesn't exist, and I'm her watchdog."

"But you saved the old man from being rubbed out, and it's logical for you to ask questions about the man who tried it."

There was another logical reason for my being interested in the dead man. He had to have remembered me without pleasure. If, like the first time, he hadn't been traveling alone, it was just possible there was someone floating around who might think there was an account to settle with me.

I must have knocked three times, each one a little more urgent, on the door of the Duchess's rooms before she opened it to me. I had the instant impression that I had caught her off-guard for the first time since I'd known her. She looked done in. She leaned against the door jamb as if she needed help.

"You okay?" I asked her.

She gave me a thin smile. "I need my beauty sleep," she said. "Come in, Daniel." She never abbreviates my name. I'm always "Daniel"; Dick Carson is always "Richard." Only Chips gets his nickname, perhaps because nobody remembers what his real name is, if they ever knew it.

I went into that junk-pile of a living room. The Duchess closed the door and dropped down on a armchair near it, not bothering to remove a small stack of magazines.

"I get you something?" I asked. "Drink?"

She shook her head. "I've spent my life being ready for anything at anytime of day or night," she said. "A long life, Daniel. But—since Will has been gone—I have a tendency to—to run out of gas."

"You do marvelously," I said. "Did you check out your jewelry?"

"Nothing missing," she said.

"You keep a list, an inventory?"

She looked at me as if I were a not-very-bright child. "Each piece has a special significance for me," she said. "The day Will gave it to me, the occasion for the gift. If a single piece were missing, a whole section of my memories would be torn away with it. I think I'd know without looking if something were gone."

"You have a safe for it, or a lock box, or what?"

I didn't altogether trust her psychic powers. I didn't really believe our hit-man had found his way into her rooms to lift her jewelry. He must, I told myself, have been looking for something else, something that related to the late Wilfred Krider, or Krider Industries.

"There was a strange and wonderful feeling of security being involved with Will Krider," she said. "He could reach out and destroy anybody in any part of the world—like swatting a fly. No one would steal from him or anyone connected with him. Retribution would come, swift and certain. We traveled all over the world, and I never put any jewelry in a hotel safe. Will would have destroyed a whole city if anyone had stolen something from him or me."

"That guy downstairs tried to steal his life ten years ago," I said.

"Thanks to you he failed," she said. "That was a bad time. I was so frightened for him, and he was so sure of you." She made more of an effort than I could remember seeing and stood up. She walked a little unsteadily across the cluttered room, beckoning to me.

Would you believe that in all the time I'd cared for her, and before, when the old man was still alive, I had never seen her bedroom. It was like walking out of a junkyard into the boudoir of some fabulous French courtesan. There was a huge, king-sized double bed, canopied, pink silk sheets, a beautiful crocheted cover. There was a dressing table, Florentine, I guessed by the carving, with a mirror behind it, circled with lights like an actress's dressing-table mirror. Neatly placed on that table were bottles and jars of creams and lotions, silver-backed hair brushes, nail buffers, every kind of beautician's aid you could imagine. Lying loosely to one side were jewels, not even kept in a box or case—enough, I imagined, to get New York City out of hock.

But I didn't spend any time studying them. On a far wall was a life-sized Botticelli-like oil painting of a lush, totally nude lady. It had been done by an extremely good artist without a hint of pornography about it. I realized it had to be the Duchess, long ago.

"It's rather pointless now," the lady said, noticing that I was riveted on the painting. "But Will loved it, had it painted when we were in Italy. He liked it hung there, and this was his room as much as mine. I—I've just not wanted to take it down."

"Did he chain the artist to a post while he painted it?" I asked.

"Flatterer!" she said. "I wasn't bad, was I?" She sounded just a touch sad, I thought. Bad! She had been magnificent. No wonder Wilfred Krider had lost his mind and heart to her. "The jewelry," she said. "I just keep it as you see it there."

"A temptation to the whole world," I said.

"The whole world doesn't come into this room, Daniel. Only Mildred, the maid. Nothing has ever been missing."

I sensed, somehow, that she didn't want me to go, despite her obvious fatigue. She sat down at the dressing table and sat staring at herself in the mirror. There was still a kind of aristocratic beauty in the aged face, despite the lines and wrinkles. The fine bone structure was still there, the eyes still had the shine of life in them, nothing compressed or tight-lipped about the mouth. She was something!

"I don't want to keep you from that beauty sleep," I said.

"But there are things I need to ask you, things the troopers need to know."

She didn't turn, but she looked up at my reflection in the mirror, standing behind her. I told her what Dr. Chance had told us downstairs. "The reason nobody heard a shot tonight is because our friend was killed at least two days ago."

"Don't call him 'our friend,' Daniel," she said. "He tried to kill Will ten years ago. Whatever he was here for on Monday it was not to fix my TV set."

"Why was he here, Duchess?" I asked her.

She looked away from my image in the glass. "I haven't the faintest idea," she said. "We had no conversation as I told you and the Lieutenant. He said the condenser was fixed, period. He refused my offer of a tip. That was all."

"You had no idea that he was the man who tried to get at the Old Man?"

"How could I? You're the only person who ever saw him that time."

"His being here has to be connected with the Kriders," I said. "His being in your room has to be connected with Wilfred Krider."

"It doesn't make any sense to me," she said.

"I keep thinking he hoped to find something here," I said. "He wasn't a common thief or he'd have scooped up your jewelry. What do you have here, Duchess, that relates to Wilfred Krider? Letters? Diaries? Maybe some documents he asked you to keep for him?"

"Nothing," she said, her voice gone hard.

"You could be a gold mine for someone looking for information about Krider," I said.

She sat silent for a moment, staring into the glass at herself. Then she turned slowly around on the little backless bench and faced me.

"Will was a power, all over the world, as you know, Daniel. He was in danger every hour of every day. That's why you were hired—and people who did your job before you.

When I first met him he was constantly afraid that someone would try to get at him though his family. When I say he was afraid, I don't mean that he felt fear in the ordinary sense. He knew how he might be attacked. Kidnapping was a danger. His children, his grandchildren, never had any kind of a free existence. After I came into the picture he worried that I might be in danger. Because of that, Daniel, I probably know less about this life than almost anyone."

"You traveled all over the world with him."

"To be available when he needed me," she said, quietly. For just a second, her eyes flickered toward that great double bed. "I was curious at the start, curious about this man I wanted more than anything else in the whole world. I wanted to know what he was involved with, who he was maneuvering, where he was using his power, his influence. I wanted to know because I loved him and was proud of him. But very early on he made it clear that I was not to be allowed to share that part of his life."

"How can you be so close to someone and not share his problems?" I asked.

"He told me that what I didn't know I could never tell anyone," she said. "He said that sometime, somewhere, someone might try by physical violence, by torture, to force me to reveal secrets that would be damaging to him. Therefore I was to know no secrets. And to this very day, Daniel, I don't." She drew a deep breath. "It never happened, and it never mattered to me, finally, that I never shared those dark secrets, whatever they were. We made love. I enjoyed the moments we were together—thousands of moments before it ended. It was enough for me. It was all I wanted."

"He must have been quite a man," I said.

"I was past forty when I met him," she said. "Surely you must guess, Daniel, that there had been other men in my life before that."

"I imagine some of them are on the wall out there," I said, nodding toward her picture gallery.

"Will Krider made them all seem like amateurs," she said. "He was everything a woman could ask for, Daniel. Tender, gentle, thoughtful—and male. So very male. So many men are really just in love with themselves, using women to prove to themselves how great they are. Will didn't need to reassure himself. He needed love. He asked for it. I gave it to him. Thank God it was what he wanted, enough for him." She gave me a faint smile. "Oh, I have secrets about Will, but nothing that would be of interest to a common criminal, a paid killer."

I thought about all the times I had been a party to this love affair the Duchess remembered with such pleasure—and tenderness. In the years I'd guarded Wilfred Krider there had been literally hundred of nights I'd driven him down from his Camden Mountain estate to the Red Cardinal; walked through a service area with him and up a back stairway to the second floor, my hand closed over the gun in my uniform jacket pocket, waited for the Duchess to answer his knock, received her pleasant "Good evening, Daniel," watched the old man disappear into the safety of her cluttered room. Then I'd go down and wait in the gardens on the far side of the pool. It could be a short time or it could be hours. They were in their late seventies and early eighties in those days. I told myself that sex must be a thing of the distant past for them, although maybe it wasn't. Certainly, visiting her was a way the Old Man could relax, unwind. When the visit was over the Duchess would appear at the window, there'd be the flutter of a handkerchief, and I'd head back to the service area, up the back stairway, and knock on her door. They would have said their good-byes in private, and when I knocked he would step out into the hall and I would take him to the car and drive him home.

Would you believe that over the years we never met anyone in the service area or on those back stairs? I was never told, but I was certain Dick Carson was alerted when Krider was coming and made sure he wouldn't encounter anyone. Secret visits that the whole staff knew about, I think. If they whispered among themselves about this strange love affair, those whispers never surfaced. It was a secret everyone shared—and kept.

I hated to leave the Duchess with nothing added to my stock of knowledge. There had to be an explanation for the presence of the man Folwell had called "Mr. X" in these rooms, but the Duchess offered nothing helpful. Mr. X had stolen nothing, had no conversation about anything with her beyond the non-existent problem with her television set. Yet his presence had to have something to do with Wilfred Krider, I had to think. Wilfred had been dead for five years, Mr. X since Monday. Neither of them could provide any answers.

"You're not writing a book, are you, dear?" I asked the Duchess.

"Good lord, no!" she said.

"There's been so much written about Wilfred Krider," I said. "Krider Industries, power struggles, revolutions, toppled governments. But nobody, so far as I know, has written anything about Wilfred Krider, the private man, the human being. You would be a prime source of information for someone who wanted to do it, if you didn't yourself. I haven't seen anyone hanging around you who looks like a writer, but—" I shrugged. "But as I suggested before, there could be diaries, documents, special information that you would have."

"I'm not writing a book," she said, "and I'm not helping someone write a book. There are no diaries or documents." She got up and walked toward the sitting room. She reached out to steady herself on the back of an armchair, something I'd never seen her do before. "I've saved all these newspapers and magazines from back over the years. Can't you guess why, Daniel? They all contain items and articles about Will, about Krider Industries, about the Krider family. But there's nothing private for anyone to risk stealing. What's here can be found in the back issues of *The New York Times* and the various magazines. All public stuff."

I was forcing her to reveal her physical limitations by

staying so long. I felt like a heel. I reached out and touched her shoulder.

"Get that beauty sleep, darlin'. But if anything at all occurs to you that will help explain what that creep was doing in your rooms, it would help a lot."

She turned to look at me, her eyes warm. "Thanks, Daniel," she said. "Thanks for being here. Will Krider knew what a good man you are. I'm grateful to him, and eternally grateful to you for being all he thought you were."

I bent down and kissed her on the cheek, something I'd never done before. "Pleasantest job I ever had," I said.

The sky had a reddish glow in the east when I got back down stairs. "Red in the morning, Sailor take warning." Captain Folwell had left the lounge, but Sergeant Lacey was there with another trooper who had set up a tape recorder on a table and was prepared with a stenotype machine. The inquisition of the Red Cardinal's guests was about to begin. Who had seen something? Who had heard something—tonight, last Monday? Some instant-color photos had been taken of the dead man. That frozen leer on his face, the matted hair, made him look like something out of a horror movie. I wouldn't have recognized the man I'd seen ten years ago from those pictures.

"The Captain's searching the catacombs," Lacey told me. "He thinks the body may have been hidden down there since Monday."

The "catacombs" was a staff name for the basement areas of the Red Cardinal. I'd been down there a few times over the years. The inn itself, like a lot of old structures, rambled over the ground on which it was built. Its builders, in the days of the Revolution, hadn't bothered to make it come out level. All ground floor rooms were on different levels, two steps up here, two steps down there. The catacombs were the same, up and down. The most notable feature was the thickness of the walls, built of stone and concrete. They were two or three feet thick, intended to last forever. It could have been built as a bomb shelter, but there'd been no bombs then, only some remote danger from British cannon. But it was like a maze, corridors leading into darkness. The part that had been made into a kitchen, bakery, freezing compartments, storage areas for food and wine were very modern with a stainless steel serving table, both a gas and electric range, a baking oven, an electric dumbwaiter that carried dining room orders to the floor above. Highly efficient. But rambling off from this center of activity were some dark corridors-storage rooms for junk, a tool shop, furnace rooms, inside oil tanks. It was a far out chance, I thought, but it wasn't impossible that a body could have been cached in one of those obscure rooms for days without being found, unless someone went exploring for some reason. There was a one-floor, flat bed elevator leading up to the parking lot area behind the inn. An iron bar raised two old fashioned cellar doors when it went up. It was used to carry heavy trash and garbage cans up to where a pickup truck could collect them. Those cellar doors opened not twenty yards around the corner of the building from the pool. The dead man could have been hidden in the catacombs, dragged to the lift when the kitchens were deserted, and then carried to the pool without the person doing the carrying being exposed for too long.

Dick Carson and Fritz Schlee, the head cook, were giving Folwell a guided tour of the catacombs. They hadn't come up with anything when I joined them. Fritz Schlee is a monumental fat man, a marvelous cook who obviously tastes everything he prepares. In his white chef's cap he towered over Dick and the captain. He speaks with a thick Middle-European accent of some sort, and has a permanent, white-toothed smile that looks as if it were pasted on his face. Once, long ago, he said to me:

"Strange I should find myself working here in Camden, with Kriders up the hill."

"What's so strange about that?" I asked him.

His smile suddenly looked savage. "As a boy I am run out of my country when big powers overthrow the government. Krider Industries. My family, who knows what became of them. I've never heard. The man you work for, Mr. Burton, is a butcher! And here I am, preparing delicacies for his mistress!"

That moment suddenly clicked into place in my memory. How long ago had it been? Was it before or after Mr. X had tried to get at Wilfred Krider? I was certain it was after, when the whole town was buzzing over the attempt on Krider's life. You might ask if I didn't suspect Fritz at the time, possibly of being Mr. X's accomplice who got him away. I guess I didn't because I was used to hearing cracks like that about Krider. He had his enemies which was why I'd been hired. Fritz was, and still is, the only chef Dick Carson has ever had at the Red Cardinal. I didn't suspect him then, and if he had been Mr. X's accomplice then it wasn't likely he was Mr. X's murderer now. Still, I thought, I better take that little memory out of mothballs and keep it up front.

Fritz gave me that white, pasted-on smile. "I recommend the chicken hash for breakfast, Mr. Burton," he said. "It is going to come out very well today."

He reminded me that I was hungry.

"Any luck?" I asked Captain Folwell.

"I tell Mr. Carson and the Captain," Fritz said, "that they are wasting time. This is my domain down here, my world. If you touch a woman you love, you know instantly if she has a fever. If anyone hid a body down here, in the farthest room, in the darkest corner, I would know! My instinct would tell me."

"I have to report to my superiors," Folwell said. "I have to say in my report that I looked and that I did or didn't find anything. So, I look." He turned to me. "Old lady dredge up anything for you?"

"Nothing. I'm on my way up to Krider's place. Thought I'd check out with you first?"

"Go. Come back with something," Folwell said. "We're about to start questioning five or six dozen pople who aren't going to know anything."

"Nobody's going to recognize our man from the pictures you took of the corpse," I said. "Not even his own mother. You'd do better to use one of those drawings that police artist made ten years ago."

"I find we don't have one," Folwell said.

"There's one on the wall in the study of my cottage," I said. "You're welcome to it. Help yourself."

"Your cottage locked?"

"Hell, man, we live in the country. And with all these brave state police around? I'll check back with you after I've talked to the people on the hill."

Fritz hadn't been too wrong about touching a woman you love and knowing, instantly, that she has a fever. His domain, he'd called the catacombs, and he'd know by instinct that something was wrong. A man develops certain special sensitivities about the world he lives in. The Red Cardinal Inn was not my world, though I'd spent a part of every day for the last five years in it. But most of my adult life had been involved with crime, and criminals, and if I'd had hackles, like a dog, they'd have risen at the smallest suggestion of violence. The dead Mr. X with a hole in his head was not a small suggestion.

I remember climbing up the stone steps from the catacombs to the lobby with that sensation of hackles rising strong in me. There was a killer loose somewhere, a killer who could have taken off two days ago and been in Mexico by now, but who had stayed around to move the body, for no sensible reason, and drop it in the swimming pool, at considerable risk to himself. The cop part of my thinking processes told me that the killer hadn't taken off because to disappear would point to him. That meant that he was part of the local scene, not one of the transient guests passing through Camden. A member of the Red Cardinal's staff? Some local resident who knew the geography of the inn well enough to hide a body and later dispose of it? It could be someone, I thought, whom I knew well, may have shared drinks with in the lounge; a friend or acquaintance, not a sinister stranger.

Chips had begun, a little later than usual, his cleanup of the lobby. He saw me come out of a side door from the catacombs. He seemed to have been waiting for me.

"Anything happening?" he asked.

Not Chips, I thought. There wasn't a trace of violence in this kindly, gentle man. I told him Folwell hadn't, so far, come up with anything in the basement.

"Fritz is sure nobody's been messing around down there," I said.

"The Duchess?" he asked. "Did she have anything to offer?"

"Have you ever seen that nude painting of her when she was in her prime?"

Chips nodded. "I've been privileged," he said, and smiled. "But what the hell was that guy doing up there?"

"Nothing stolen," I said. "No conversation with her. She claims she has nothing there that could be of any interest to Wilfred Krider's enemies—except stacks and stacks of newspaper stories."

"So that's what all that junk is," he said. "Newspaper stories about the Old Man."

"Easily found in the newspaper files without risking being caught in robbery."

"And without running any risk of being seen, particularly by you, Dan. You'd have recognized him as the man you shot ten years ago, wouldn't you?"

"For sure," I said. I looked around to make certain no one was close enough to hear what we were saying, "our man was killed Monday, according to Dr. Chance. The killer hid the body, waited around for two days, and then moved it. It had to be someone we know, Chips. Someone from the outside would have taken off Monday, after he hid the body. He stuck around because to go would have been to finger himself. It's ten-to-one he's still here."

"Oh, man!" Chips said.

"It could be staff," I said. "It could be some regular customer from the town. Maybe there are some guests who have been here since Monday."

Chips looked dazed behind his horn-rimmed glasses. "A small army," he said. "Look, Dan, this dead man is about six feet tall, weighed about a hundred and ninety pounds, wouldn't you say?"

I nodded.

"Can you imagine a woman dragging him somewhere to hide him and then lugging him out to the pool and dumping him? We've got eight-ten women working here—maids, hostess, waitresses, the desk, two cashiers, the gift shop, two in the kitchen. Part-time girls who substitute for the regulars, extra waitresses in the summer season, like now. Men?" He shrugged. "Two shifts a day, you know. Chef, baker, helper, dishwasher in the kitchen. Bar help. One night man on the desk, two outside men." He gave me a sour smile. "Me," he said, "and Dick."

"Regular customers?"

"Lord, Dan, that covers half the county."

"That may be what we have to do," I said.

But that wasn't anything I could do. That was a tedious police routine that faced Captain Folwell. That's why I guess I was a bad cop. Routines with all the protection built around the probably-guilty drove me off my rocker.

What I could do now that might be helpful was to visit the Krider family up on the mountain. Mr. X might very well have made some kind of contact there. It was a sure bet that his reason for being in Camden had to do with the Kriders, living or dead.

It was strange, but the "hackle" sensation was with me strongly. The lobby was beginning to buzz with people who had suddenly discovered they weren't going to be allowed to leave the Red Cardinal until they had first been interviewed by the state police. Tell people they can't go some place and it suddenly becomes imperative that they leave. Men and women were crowding around the desk, trying to check out. Rose Garner, the chief desk clerk, was trying to charm them out of their outrage. When they couldn't pay up and go, people decided to go anyway, only to find state troopers at the exits. I wondered how many of them were thinking what I was thinking—that somewhere in the center of this hassle was a killer, waiting patiently to get through the mill and take off.

I had no problem getting out. I was special. I walked across the outside lawn and across the highway to my cottage. Just as I got there a trooper came out the kitchen way. He was carrying the old police-artist drawing of Mr. X.

"The Captain said it was alright to go in and get it," the trooper said.

"My pleasure," I said.

"He looks better in this than he does in the morgue," the trooper said.

"The difference between being alive and dead," I said.

I was still wearing the safari jacket I'd had on for last evening's sojourn in the bar. Laura Stark told me she liked it—thought I looked handsome—like Richard Chamberlain. I decided to wear it more often.

A look in the bathroom mirror told me I needed a shave. I managed that, threw on a pair of jeans and a sports shirt. I had an electric percolator I keep going in the kitchen. It had been on a long time now and the coffee tasted bitter, but it helped.

I got my little yellow Volkswagen out of the garage and headed up Camden Mountain. It was like going home. I'd lived there for ten years while I watched over Wilfred Krider, but I hadn't been inside the grounds since his funeral five years ago. I had never gotten along well with Maxwell Krider, or his son Joshua. To them I'd been a paid intruder, always in the way of their privacy. I hadn't given a damn for anyone but the Old Man when I'd lived there so their hostility hadn't bothered me then. It wasn't going to help the going this morning, however.

Hilltop was the not-very-imaginative name on the gate post at the entrance to the estate. But the place was changed now. In the old days there had been two heavy iron gates, always closed. There was a stone gatehouse, and there had always been a man there, armed with an automatic rifle. No more. The gates were open, the gatehouse unmanned. In the old days, nobody ever drove through those gates till the gate man had made a phone call to the house. I drove in now, as though it were a public park.

Wilfred Krider had loved this place. He had built it out of stone and Vermont marble. It stood on the side of the mountain, looking directly up the valley towards miles and miles of hills. It looked like a palace—or a fortress. I guess the old man had meant it to be both. There were a couple of acres of lawn, shrubs, and gardens, manicured to the teeth, as you drove up the crushed-stone driveway to the porticoed front door. In the old days, the squad of gardeners who did the manicuring carried guns.

In the old days, a couple of Dobermans cruised the grounds at night, ready to take your arm off if you'd found a way to climb the electrified fence. There had been one other dog when I lived there who belonged to the Old Man, a joyous and active golden retriever. As I got out of my VW I saw what looked like a lumpy doormat stretched out on the lawn. As I walked toward it a head raised up, ears moved but the dog, because it was a dog, made no effort to get up. The muzzle was grey, the eyes watery.

"Jock?" I said.

A tail thumped against the grass. I'd supposed old Jock

was long dead. It turned out the two lives the Old Man had cared most about, Martha Walton and Jock, were still hanging in there. I knelt down beside him.

"Well, boy, you've gotten a little bit long in the tooth," I said. I rubbed his head and a rough old tongue licked my hand.

"I don't suppose a man who likes dogs can be all bad," a sardonic voice said.

I looked up and saw Josh Krider standing just outside the front door. Joshua Krider is the Old Man's grandson, Maxwell Krider's son. You have to get the generation gaps straight. Wilfred Krider had been eighty-four when he died, that would make his son, Maxwell, about sixty, and Josh in his early thirties. Josh had been kicked out of prep school the year I first came to work at *Hilltop* for the Old Man. He was later kicked out of a couple of colleges. He was a boozer, a womanizer, a creep—for my money. I suppose a psychiatrist would say he had lived in a constant state of rebellion against his grandfather. The iron gates, the electric fence, the bodyguards who went places with him to guard against the constant danger of kidnapping, deprived him of any freedom of movement, any casual association with friends outside of Wilfred Krider's world. When he went away to school he broke all the rules, a way of thumbing his nose at the rules that were imposed on him at home. As far as I know he'd never had a job, or dreamed of any career. He didn't have to. Maxwell supplied him with money and would bail him out of any trouble he got into. He hated me because I'd imposed certain restrictions on him when I worked there. At the Old Man's funeral he had said to me, "Thank God, you won't be around to give orders any more, Buster!"

The Krider men were vaguely alike. The Old Man had been rugged, muscular, like carved out of rock on the face of a mountain. Maxwell, living most of his life in a wheel chair because of a childhood bout with polio, was the same figure, but painted somehow by a timid watercolorist. Josh was the Old Man again, but done by a caricaturist with a wicked sense of humor. His contempt for other people and the world around him gave Josh the look, at least to me, of a young and evil gargoyle.

"What the hell are you doing here, Burton?" he asked.

"I need to talk to you and your father," I said.

I still knelt beside old Jock while he gently licked my hand.

"You've come to tell us that old bag down at the inn has finally given up the ghost?" His mouth was drawn down at the corners, his slate-grey eyes narrowed.

I patted the dog and stood up. Old Jock whimpered.

"Miss Walton is fine," I said. "But there's been a murder at the Red Cardinal and it may be a matter of concern to you."

"I can't imagine how, unless it was that creep Chips who's kicked me out of the bar a couple of times.

"The man who was murdered," I said, "is the man who, ten years ago, tried to knock off your grandfather."

Josh gave me a wry smile. "I've never forgiven you for that, Burton," he said. "If you'd just been in the hay with one of the housemaids that morning—let's see, it was the one named Elsi you were making out with in those days, wasn't it?—we'd all have gotten out of this jail a hell of a lot sooner. So the guy is dead. What's that got to do with us?"

"That's what I'm here to ask," I said. "Where is your father?"

"Having breakfast on the terrace with my old lady," he said. "I don't imagine that murder with his poached egg will improve his digestion."

I didn't wait for him to lead the way. I knew where the terrace was. Wilfred Krider had been having his breakfast out there the morning that Mr. X tried to get him.

The old dog got up to follow me. He must have limped in front of Josh because Josh kicked him out of the way and the dog cried out and rolled over on the grass.

I caught his arm and brought it up hard against his back. "You're sick," I muttered in his ear. I applied pressure on his thumb, until he started gasping and went down on his knees. I released him and waited for him to get up, but he just stayed there, holding his arm and panting. I leaned down and patted the dog. I felt good.

Maxwell Krider and his wife, Eleanore, were on the terrace. Lampert, the houseman who had been there in my time, saw me before they did. Lampert must be as old as God, I thought, but he still can serve a poached egg with a kind of old world elegance. He gave me a surprised smile. He had always been a friend.

"Good morning Mrs. Krider, Mr. Krider," I said.

Maxwell was in his wheel chair, a lightweight rug over his knees. He gave me a startled look.

"Burton!" he said. "You remember Burton, Eleanore?"

We'd always gotten along well. I think she was the only member of the family Wilfred Krider had really cared for. She was probably in her early fifties, quite beautiful in a frail way. I suspect that life with a crippled and probably impotent husband and that weirdo son had aged her too soon.

"Won't you join us with some coffee?" she asked.

I said I'd like it. Lampert brought a chair for me and went to the sideboard for coffee.

"I don't imagine you've come just to pass the time of day, Burton," Maxwell said. "Miss Walton?"

"Miss Walton is fine, if a little shaken up," I said. I told them why I was there. Maxwell's pale face looked as though he smelled something bad.

"So at last we know who he is," he said.

"Not yet," I said. "He wasn't carrying any identification. The troopers have taken his fingerprints, of course. Maybe something will come of that, but not so far."

"A criminal," Maxwell said. "He must have a record of some sort. You haven't said who killed him."

"We don't know. That's one of the reasons I'm here."

"I don't understand," Maxwell said.

"Miss Walton found this Mr. X in her rooms on Monday

morning. He passed himself off as a television repair man. We now know that he was killed shortly after that, his body hidden for two days, and then dumped in the swimming pool about one o'clock this morning. All we know about this man is that, ten years ago, he tried to kill your father. A paid hit-man we thought at the time. He comes back and breaks into Miss Walton's rooms — a connection with your father. What was his next move going to be? This man's interest in Camden has to be Kriders. Your father? You?"

"Me!" Maxwell looked startled.

"Something about your father. Something he thought Miss Walton might know — something about him he thought he might find in her rooms. When he didn't find it I'm guessing his next move would have been here. Unless he had already been here — ?"

"Been here? What nonsense!"

"Look, Mr. Krider. You wouldn't have known who he was if he'd come here to talk to you," I said. "Did some stranger come here to ask you questions about your father?"

"No!"

"He could have posed as anything, a newspaper reporter, a historian, even someone connected with Krider Industries. You're not active in the business. He could have passed himself off as someone connected with one of the Krider corporations, asking what seemed like perfectly legitimate questions."

"There's been no one here asking about father — not since five years ago when the man who wrote *Blood And Power* came here to do some research on him."

"Not recently? Not three or four days ago? He didn't get the answer he wanted from you and went rummaging around in Miss Walton's rooms for it."

"How many times do I have to tell you, Burton, there's been nobody here to ask anything." The color had drained out of Maxwell's face.

"Blackmail." I said.

"What are you talking about?"

"Has somebody been blackmailing you over the years since your father died?"

His hands closed tightly over the metal arms of his wheel chair. "I think I've had about enough of this, Burton," he said.

"The police are going to ask you all of these questions," I said. "I owe your father. He'd want me to help if I could."

"The police will get the same answers from me that I've given you," Maxwell said. "No strangers posing as anything. No blackmail."

Eleanore Krider leaned forward in her chair. "Whatever this man was after, Dan, he didn't get it. Someone stopped him."

"I know," I said. "Ten years ago he was out to get Wilfred Krider. We stopped him. Three days ago I have to believe he was out to try to damage the Kriders again. He was stopped. Stopping him may have protected the Kriders. Mr. Krider could call on all the resources his father had. If you stopped this man, Mr. Krider, and you'll tell me why, I might just be willing to play your side of the street."

"The whole notion is absurd," Maxwell said. "I stopped nobody from doing anything. I don't know of any damage anybody could do me. If I did I wouldn't use my father's tactics. That's part of another world, long gone."

"I wonder if it is, Mr. Krider," I said. "From what I read in the papers about the world today I very much doubt it."

"If someone thought they were protecting us by eliminating this man, Dan, who could it be?" Eleanore Krider asked.

"That, Mrs. Krider, is the sixty-four dollar question," I said. "What friend do you have who would commit a murder for you?"

"That will be just about it!" Maxwell said.

There comes a point in any interrogation when, as a trained cop, you know you aren't going to make it. I stood up, aware that I hadn't touched the coffee Lampert had brought me.

"I may have guessed all wrong, Mr. Krider," I said. "But

at least you've been warned that a killer was interested in you. Ten years ago he had a friend. He may still have."

I walked around the corner of the house toward my car. I wasn't alone. Eleanore Krider had followed me. She slipped her arm through mine and we walked toward the yellow Volkswagen. Old Jock, the retriever, was sitting by the car, his tongue lolling out the side of his mouth.

"It was nice of you to come, Dan," Eleanore Krider said.

I might as well tell it here. After I'd been working for Krider about a year, Eleanore and I had a thing for each other. She was a beauty, unhappy in her marriage, and I was a lonely, hungry man. For a brief interval our little romance had all the delicious excitement of the secret and the forbidden. Somehow the Old Man got wind of what was going on between Eleanore and me, and spiked it. I must drop the lady or he would put me through his special meat grinder. There really wasn't any choice, and so that was that.

"I doubt I'll be welcome again," I said. "I tangled with Josh on the way in. He kicked the old dog. I didn't like it."

"Is he hurt?" she asked.

"He might have a sprained thumb or a sore arm," I said.

"Oh, Dan," she said. Her fingers tightened on my arm. "You really think Maxwell can be in some kind of trouble?"

"There has to be a connection between the dead man and the Kriders," I said.

"Maxwell has never had anything to do with Krider Industries," she said. "But after Father Krider died there were lots of people here, business associates, looking for records, documents, tapes, anything that Father Krider might have kept here that related to the Krider empire."

"Something particular?"

"I don't know, Dan. Nobody ever talked to me. Maxwell never discussed it with me." A bitterness crept into her voice. "Maxwell and I never talk about anything but the weather, and what he wants for lunch, and how badly *my* son has turned out. But things have changed since you lived here, Dan. The electric fence is gone, the gates stand open, there are no men with guns. We're free to come and go. Only nobody comes, and there's no place to go. Oh, Dan, I wish—I wish, I wish, I wish!"

"It wouldn't have worked," I said. "The Old Man would have steamrollered us both. Something out of the past has come back, though, Eleanore."

"Something dangerous, you think?"

"One man is already dead," I said. I stopped and looked down at her. "Why don't you just get on your bicycle and take off? Josh doesn't need you. Maxwell could make out his own lunch menus, couldn't he?"

"It's too late," she said. "Everything in life seems to come too late. You came too late, fourteen years ago."

"You need me, just yell," I said. "If you have strange visitors, anyone from Krider Industries asking questions, let me know. I wouldn't like to see you in trouble just because you live here."

"Thank you, Dan." She took a deep breath and disengaged her arm from mine. "It's nice to know that you're only just down the hill from here."

We reached the car and I opened the door. Without any invitation from me, Jock, the old dog, jumped in ahead of me.

Eleanore gave me a bright, hard look. "He wants to escape, too, doesn't he?" she said. "Take him if you want, Dan. He knows he can trust you. After what happened with Josh he's not likely to survive here very long."

I drove away, feeling slightly idiotic. I'd found out nothing, I'd acquired a dog. I took a sidewise glance at the old retriever, who looked absurdly happy, and remembered the sign on the screen door into the Red Cardinal's lobby. NO BARE FEET, NO PETS.

"You asked for it, Jocko," I said to the dog.

I'm not a record keeper. I worked for Wilfred Krider for ten years, made three trips abroad with him, lived with him the majority of the time behind his electric fence on Camden Mountain. My job was to keep him safe, not to inquire into his business affairs. I carried a gun and stayed close to him. The enormous complexities of Krider Industries were no concern of mine. Early on I would ask the Old Man what something was all about, and he'd give me his ice cold stare and say, "You don't need to know that, Daniel." I stopped asking. What I was told I never forgot. I never forgot telephone numbers, or names, or addresses, if they mattered. I have a photographic memory for faces, which is how I was able to give the police artist such an exact description of Mr. X ten years ago. In all that time no one had ever identified him from the drawing. I knew from seeing him dead this morning how exact that drawing, from my memory of our shootout, had been.

"The human mind is like a computer," Krider used to say. "Put in garbage and you'll get garbage out. Don't clutter your mind, Daniel, with things that don't matter."

Mr. X mattered, but it hadn't been my job to find him in the last ten years. That had been a police job and a job for the special security force of Krider Industries. Neither of them had succeeded. Captain Folwell was back at it. There was another man who should be. His name was Mark Stone, and he was head of security for Krider Industries.

Stone is a remarkable man. Security for Krider isn't a handful of cops with night sticks. It's a small army of experts, former FBI agents, former CIA agents, military men who train revolutionary forces in distant countries, demolition experts. Mark Stone's people could fight a war if it benefited Krider. Maybe they have. Today's multi-national corporations are nations in themselves. I met Stone the day after Mr. X tried to get Krider. He came to Camden, summoned there by the Old Man. Questions: Who is Mr. X? Who hired him to kill?

Stone is a rock-faced man, Brooks Brothers-dressed, who looks like a business executive out of a movie. The Old Man told me he speaks a half a dozen languages including Arabic and Hebrew. Stone knows, I was told, everything there is to know about the power structures in our society.

On his visit to Camden, Stone treated me exactly like what I was, a gunman hired to protect the Old Man. He listened to the details of my encounter with Mr. X, examined the tire tracks and footprints that indicated an accomplice, said, "Thank you," to me, and that was all I saw of him.

Wilfred Krider talked about him later, however. The Old Man was disturbed by what had happened. How had Mr. X gotten through the gates, past the gate man with the automatic rifle, or over the electric fence? A carefully set up system had broken down, and if I hadn't caught Mr. X actually breaking into the house Wilfred Krider's number would have been up. I knew the other guards inside the grounds, the armed gateman, were Stone's men.

The Old Man let his hair down to me a few days after Stone's visit, with no lead to Mr. X or his employers having developed. It was a rare occasion.

"Do you know, Daniel, why I hired you when I had my own security people, Mark Stone's people?" he asked me. We were sitting together on the terrace at *Hilltop*.

"You can't have too much protection, I guess," I said.

"You can't have enough protection you can *trust,*" he said.

That surprised me. "You don't trust Stone and his men?"

"They are the best-trained, most efficient, toughest body of men I know of," the Old Man said. He sat silent for a moment, staring out at the distant hills. "I'm getting old, Daniel. There are people who have been my friends, my lieutenants, who are impatient for me to move over and let them have their turn at the controls."

"You're saying your own people might be out to get you?"

"The lust for power is a disease, Daniel," he said. "I have it. I would crush my closest friend if he tried to steal power from me. Over the years I have made men very rich, given them power in their own areas. But soon—not too soon, I hope—I will have run my race. There may be those who don't want to wait."

"But Stone and his men are your people, your team," I said.

"Mark Stone may have had a vision," the Old Man said.

"A vision?"

"Of who will succeed me. It may have been pointed out to him that he'd be well-advised to side with someone who is planning to take my place."

"Are you saying the man I shot may have been working for Stone?"

"He got into the grounds here, Daniel, past Stone's men. If it hadn't been for you—." He brought his fist down on the arm of his chair. "He may not have been working for Stone, but Stone could have been persuaded to have his men look the other way."

"But who is this—this pretender?" I asked.

The Old Man shrugged. "It could be any one of *ten* men in the structure of Krider Industries who is breathing hard, waiting for his moment. Stone may have made a judgment and decided on which side his bread is buttered."

That was the one time the Old Man talked freely to me about what he feared. Five years went by, however, and there was no new attempt on his life. I found myself watching the men who were supposed to protect him, but no one made any kind of suspicious move. I decided Krider's fears had been unfounded. When he came to the end of the line there was no violence. His old heart gave out while he was jogging.

I drove into the yard of my cottage. Across the road there were still a half a dozen police cars parked around the Red Cardinal. Jocko, the dog, followed me into the house as though he'd lived there all his life. I got a mixing bowl out of the pantry and filled it with water, put it down under the kitchen sink. Jocko slurped around in it, looked satisfied, and followed me into the living room. I sat down at my desk and Jocko curled up on the rug at my feet. He was at home.

I dialed a number I had never called before in my life. It had been in that special memory bank for phone numbers for fifteen years, kept there in case of emergency.

An impersonal operator's voice answered. "Mark Stone's office."

"I'd like to speak to Mr. Stone," I said. "My name is Dan Burton. In case he's forgotten who I am, remind him that I used to work for Wilfred Krider."

"I'll see if Mr. Stone is in," the voice said.

I waited what seemed like five minutes, and then Stone came on the line.

"Of course I remember you, Burton. What can I do for you?"

"The guy we were looking for here in Camden ten years ago turned up in the middle of the night," I said.

"So you've finally identified him?"

"He turned up dead," I said. I gave him a quick but detailed account of the reappearance of Mr. X.

"No lead to the killer?" Stone asked. He doesn't have a shred of emotion in his flat, level voice. No surprise. No real curiosity. I wondered if he were the self-serving bastard the Old Man had suspected he might be. I wondered who gave him his orders these days.

"Not as of an hour ago," I said.

"What do you want of me, Burton? Finding the killer is a police job, not mine."

"Let's start over again," I said. I was starting to simmer a little. "You know who Miss Walton is?"

"Yes."

"You know what she was to Wilfred Krider?"

"Yes."

"Mr. X paid a visit to her room."

"Mr. X, I take it, is your name for the man we were looking for ten years ago."

"For want of a better name," I said. "He came here ten years ago to kill the Old Man. He comes back after ten years and is found snooping around in Miss Walton's rooms. I'd have to be an idiot not to assume his being here is connected with the Kriders. Who else would I ask about that?"

"As I understand it, Wilfred Krider left you a legacy on condition you'd look out for Miss Walton's safety and well-being."

"That's the way it is."

"So what are you doing about this?"

"Miss Walton found the man in her rooms, had no conversation with him. He said he was there to fix her TV set. There's nothing missing in her rooms. She says there was nothing there relating to the Old Man except a mass of newspaper clippings. I've talked to Maxwell Krider. No one's approached him. He says he has nothing to do with Krider Industries."

"The truth," Stone said.

"So I called you. If anyone can guess what this is all about it has to be you. Years and years behind the scenes!"

There were three beats of silence, and then he said: "Well, thanks for calling."

And that was that.

A secret and devious man, Mark Stone. As secret and devious as the CIA where I suspect he got his training. If he chose to interest himself in Mr. X or Mr. X's killer I might never know about it. Folwell might never know about it.

Krider Industries, through Mark Stone, could settle their own account, if this was an account of theirs, and the law, the community, the other people involved would never know they'd lifted a finger. Successful violence is not good advertising for the big boys, but it's good business—good Big Business. If our little private murder in a little country inn did involve the Kriders, as I suspected, then I'd done the right thing in alerting Stone. If I was wrong about the theme music then I'd done no harm. Stone would ignore the whole thing.

I knew I should report back to Folwell, even though I had nothing to make him happy. I also had thoughts about Fritz's chicken hash. I'd been on the go, without sleep, for twenty-four hours and I'd had nothing to eat since a small steak and a green salad at last night's dinner.

I got up to go, and Jocko prepared to go with me.

"Sorry, kid," I told him. "No pets across the street. Settle down and I'll try to scare up some food for you before I come back."

I left him looking a little hurt and walked across the street to the Red Cardinal. The trooper stationed at the front entrance let me into bedlam. The lobby was crowded with people and luggage. Folwell was evidently being slow and methodical about his interrogation. Everyone seemed to have a priority for wanting to go *now,* a plane to catch, an appointment to keep. Folwell, set up in the lounge, was taking them one by one, or at least family by family. He wasn't to be hurried.

Dick Carson, smiling cheerfully, was circulating among his disgruntled guests, trying to persuade them, I imagine, that the police and not the Red Cardinal were responsible for their discomfort. There was free brunch in the dining room. That is known as trying to leave a good taste in the mouths of unhappy customers.

Someone took me by the arm. It was Chips.

"Anything helpful?" he asked.

"I've now inherited a dog," I said. "No, nothing helpful."

"The Duchess has been trying to reach you," he said. "She's been calling the desk every ten minutes, asking for you."

She might have come up with something, I thought. "Tell Folwell I'm not ducking him," I said to Chips. "But nothing from the Kriders."

I edged my way through the crowd to the stairway to the second floor. Looking at the crowd I realized Folwell had a long way to go.

After some delay the Duchess opened her door a crack, and then wide.

"Where the hell have you been?" she asked.

"Visiting the Kriders," I said. "Something wrong, or did you find something?" I stepped into the world of disorder.

She closed the door and stood leaning against it. "I couldn't tell the police. They'd laugh at me," she said.

"I doubt they'd have the nerve," I said. "What is it, Duchess?"

She drew a deep breath and her painted eyelids seemed to flutter. "Someone has kidnapped Teddy," she said.

Oh brother, I thought, the time has come when she isn't going to make sense anymore. It could happen overnight, I supposed. Still she was fond of overstatement.

"Ransom demand?" I asked, trying to kid her.

"Not yet," she said, sounding grim. She was serious, for God sake!

"So when—and how?" I asked her.

"Last night—or this morning, that is—when I came downstairs to the President's Room to talk to Lieutenant Folwell—after I saw the TV repair man in the pool."

She had most of it wrong, of course. Folwell is a captain, there is no President's Room, and there was no TV repair man. Once she had made up her mind to something that's the way it stayed.

"I didn't bring Teddy down with me then, because, as I said at the time, he doesn't like strangers—particularly hostile strangers."

"So you left him here?" I said, trying to play along.

She nodded. "It—it wasn't pleasant down there, Daniel. The dead man. That—that awful grin on his face; the place where the bullet went into his head. I—I have a pretty strong stomach but that was a little much!"

"I know. It turned me off too, dear."

"When I came back up here I didn't look for Teddy. I knew he was here—somewhere." She waved at the piles of disorder. "I lay down for a while. I must have slept a little, I guess. Then, this morning was different from the usual routine. Normally I take Teddy for a walk at a quarter to nine. Mildred comes in while I'm out to make my bed and clean the rooms. This morning I decided to skip the walk and I didn't let Mildred in at the usual time. You came up to ask me questions. Would you believe that all that time I didn't look for Teddy? I mean, he's a good luck charm but he isn't really real, you know. Finally I decided to go downstairs to see what was going on, I looked for Teddy, but I couldn't find him anywhere."

I gestured around at the piles of newspapers, magazines, and junk. "He could be misplaced under something," I said.

"He's gone, Daniel. He's not here. The only time I've been gone out of these rooms since the last time I had him, was as I told you, when I went downstairs to talk to the Lieutenant after I'd seen the body in the pool. Someone had to have come in here then and taken Teddy." I thought she was close to tears. "How could I have ignored him, not looked for him when I came back? Fifty years—he's been with me every moment of every day—except that trip downstairs to—to view the body."

"Did you lock your door when you went downstairs?" I asked. "I was with you, but I don't recall if you did."

"It's not a lock like the doors on the other rooms," she said. "It's a Yale lock. It locks itself when you pull the door to."

"Mildred must have a special key—not the regular pass key she uses for other rooms."

"Yes, she does. And they keep a spare at the front desk, in case I should forget my key and lock myself out."

"Well, let's look around—just in case you've got Teddy covered up with something," I said.

"He's not here, Daniel!"

She was really telling me not to disturb anything. My cop's mind was beginning to puzzle at it. In the next room, lying loose on the dressing table, were thousands of dollars worth of rings, bracelets, necklaces. Why would anyone break in here and steal a teddy bear, a fifty-year-old teddy bear not worth a nickel to anyone but the Duchess? And when you asked that question you went back to Monday morning? What had Mr. X been doing here while she was out for her morning walk? Her jewels had been left untouched, there was nothing else except newspapers and magazines that had no value to anyone except the Duchess. It was crazy, but Teddy hadn't been there that morning. The Duchess was carrying him when she came back into the rooms from her walk and found the "TV repair man" there. Could he have been interested in the faded old toy bear? Why, for God sake? He hadn't tried to grab it from her then. And he hadn't come back for it. He had been dead for two days before Teddy was missed. The phantom accomplice who had helped Mr. X escape ten years ago? Was he here in the Red Cardinal playing some kind of cockeyed game with an ancient toy? None of it made the slightest sense.

"Let me talk to Mildred, the maid," I said. "She may have seen someone coming or going."

"Teddy was here at two o'clock this morning," the Duchess said, "When I went down to talk to the Lieutenant about the murder. Mildred isn't on at night, so she couldn't have seen anybody come or go while I was being questioned downstairs. That's when it had to happen, Daniel. Teddy was here when I went down—when you came up to get me, hooked my dress. Teddy was here then."

"When you came back upstairs you didn't look for him," I said. "He could have been here then, taken later."

"I haven't been out of these rooms since then. The only person who's come in here between then and now is you—

earlier this morning, to check on whether any jewelry had been taken."

"You think I may have picked Teddy up and forgotten about it?"

"Don't be an ass, Daniel," she said. "I'm telling you that he was taken while I was being interrogated by the police!"

"So to get in here without leaving signs of breaking and entering," I said, "the thief had to have gotten hold of your key, Mildred's key, or the spare key from the front desk," I said. I took a look at the door lock. There was no sign of its having been forced. "Unless of course you didn't pull it shut when we went downstairs, after I'd hooked up your dress," I said. "Not forced, luv."

"Of course I pulled it shut! I always pull it shut! Do I remember? Of course I don't. When something is routine you only remember not doing it. I don't remember not doing it."

I had to admit there was a kind of logic to that. So why would somebody take Teddy? I remembered holding him one night in the bar when she had to go to the john. His eyes weren't diamonds, they were shoe buttons. I could vouch for that. His second hide, provided by F.A.O. Schwarz a couple of decades ago, was worn thin in places. He was valuable only to a lady who had sentimental and romantic associations with him. In today's world we see repeated acts of malicious vandalism. It's become almost a way of life in our time. Did somebody have it in for the old girl and know how distressed she would be if she lost her good luck charm? I stood looking at her griefstricken face. I couldn't recall ever hearing anyone in the Red Cardinal, the staff with whom she had daily dealings, make a single sour remark about her. Oh, they had sometimes laughed at her clothes, speculated about her long-finished love life, but she had never given anyone reason to resent her. She treated the help around the inn with courtesy, with patience, even with friendliness. She never made imperious demands. I would have bet anything there wasn't a soul on the staff who had any desire to play a mean trick on her.

"Look, darlin'," I said. "I'll do what I can to find him, but I simply can't believe that anyone on the staff here would want to play a mean trick on you, or even a bad joke."

"Nor I," she said.

"Has there been anyone around the inn in the last few days that you recognize from the past, from way back sometime? Someone who may have known you and Wilfred Krider—have had something in for both of you, or one of you? Someone who knew from way back what Teddy stood for in your life?"

She shook her head, slowly. "Nobody," she said. "I sometimes think there is no one left alive who was a contemporary of Will's or mine. That's one of the unhappy things, Daniel, about getting too damned old. We never had a social life—with other people, that is. We had each other, our pleasures together, no other people."

"I'll do what I can," I said.

There had to be a rational, normal explanation for the disappearance of her faded toy. He could have toppled into a wastebasket, covered by something, carried out by Mildred without the maid's noticing. The Duchess got a new *New York Times* every day, but if there was nothing in it about Wilfred Krider she threw it out. Wilfred Krider, five years dead, was no longer news. That's a lot of daily waste paper! Teddy, I tried to convince myself, had gone out that way.

Mildred Swanson, the second-floor maid, is a big, square-jawed country woman with forearms on her like a blacksmith. She is one of the real old-timers on the staff, having gone to work for Dick and Ruth Carson very early on in their management of the inn. Her vocabulary is limited, but she can make her points with sheer volume. I have heard her shouting at young people who were just starting to work at the inn, or filling in for the summer rush, with a ferocity that would curl your hair. Things were supposed to be done at the Red Cardinal "just so" and Mildred was determined to make damn sure that nothing was left undone, overlooked, or done wrong. The Red Cardinal is her world and she is determined to keep it in orbit.

Most important at the moment was the fact that she had cared for the Duchess's rooms for almost twenty years. It was unthinkable that Mildred would steal anything, mislay anything carelessly, or play any kind of malicious trick on the old woman. I found her down the hall, cleaning out a room that had been vacated by guests who had been allowed to leave the inn by Folwell. It was a rather typical Red Cardinal room, reflecting, I suspect, Ruth Carson's impeccable taste; a four-poster bed with a candlewyck bedspread; hooked rugs on the floor; summer chintz curtains at the windows. There were books and current magazines to give the guest plenty to read. Mildred was in a mood.

"Listening to people you'd think Dick Carson had deliberately delayed them," Mildred said. "One thing for sure, they won't stop here again, and good riddance, I say. Imagine that, after a free breakfast and all!"

I told her about Teddy. She looked shocked, her face twisted in an expression of disbelief.

"You knew that our murder victim was in her rooms on Monday pretending to be a TV repair man?" I asked her. "He didn't take Teddy, though, because he was killed on Monday and Teddy was around for two days after that."

"First mistake I ever made in nineteen years and four months," Mildred said.

"How's that?" I asked.

"I let that freak into Miss Walton's room," she said. "She'd gone for her morning walk, I was just finishing her place, coming out into the hall with my vacuum and a pail and a mop. This man came along the hall and said Mr. Carson had sent him up to fix Miss Walton's TV. I didn't know him from

Adam, but in the summertime local tradespeople hire strangers to take care of the rush."

"Wouldn't Chips have been the most likely one to fix her set?" I asked.

"I suppose. But Chips has other things to do. I supposed Dick Carson had asked Willoughby's—that's the local TV genius—to send someone over. So I let this character in, God help me."

"But he didn't take anything, didn't do any harm."

"He got himself killed! That's harm enough, ain't it?"

"About Teddy," I said. "I've been guessing he might have been thrown out in the trash. She says he was there in the middle of the night, but there's been a lot of coming and going since the Duchess saw the body in the pool."

"But no trash," she said, emphatically. "I wasn't let in this morning. She asked me to skip her. Wasn't feeling too good, I guess. Poor old lady, she had to look at that corpse, didn't she? I had to look at him, too, and tell Ed Folwell he was the guy I let in, thinking he was a TV man. Damn near throwed up!"

"How do you handle the trash?" I asked her.

"I tell you, there wasn't any this morning."

"She's awfully old, Mildred. Teddy could have been missing longer than she remembers. Maybe he got in the trash yesterday."

"Let me tell you one thing, Mr. Burton. She's sharper than you and me put together. If she says he was there at the time she saw the body in the pool, then he was there. She can remember exactly what somebody said to her fifty years ago, when, and where, and what they had for supper! Don't get the idea there's anything vague about that old doll. God help me, I wouldn't for the world have anything happen to her—and I let that creep into her room!"

"So take it easy," I said. "He didn't harm her."

"For all of me he could have," she said.

"What do you do with the trash, Mildred?"

"I keep tellin' you—."

"I know, but just tell me—."

"There's like a dumbwaiter at the end of the hall," she said. "I got two big barrels there. I carry the trash out of the rooms in the baskets, empty them in the garbage cans. When the cans are full I slide them on the dumbwaiter and ring the bell. Somebody in the basement pulls down the dumbwaiter and takes off the cans. Later they're lifted out to the parking lot where the garbage truck takes them. But there's one more thing, Mr. Burton."

"Oh?"

"I don't just dump trash from those baskets into the garbage cans. I take it out, piece by piece. People are awful careless, you know? They'll drop a ring, or a watch, or something in the trash—sweep it careless off a table top. Then they can't find it and who gets the blame? The maid. The maid is always a thief when something is missing. I could have retired long ago if I'd hung onto to everything that got in the trash baskets by mistake. No, sir, Mr. Burton, I can tell you for sure. Teddy didn't go out in the trash."

You don't argue with Mildred. You don't argue, and you believe what she tells you. So Teddy's disappearance wasn't accidental. So what the hell was it, then?

The crowd in the lobby had thinned out. I guess Captain Folwell had found a way to shorten his questioning. What could he ask except had they ever seen the man in the artist's drawing and the grim after-death pictures, and had anyone heard a gunshot anywhere in the inn sometime on Monday? Evidently no one had answered "yes" to either question. Things seemed to be getting back to normal. The majority of the guests had decided not to change their plans. A lot of them were circulating in the gift shop which occupies a space at the north end of the building.

The gift shop is run by Ruth Carson's two middle-aged maiden aunts, Miss Anne and Miss Amy Quigley. Every morning the baker in the catacombs supplied the Misses Quigley with fresh-baked bread, rolls, tarts, and cakes. This brought local people in each day because you couldn't buy baked goods as good anywhere else in town. Once you were in you had a chance at jams, jellies, pickled goods, scarfs, hats, corkscrews, steak knives, dolls, maple sugar, candy, syrup, hand-crafted wooden salad bowls, knitted neckties, Red Cardinal pipe tobacco, English Country perfumes, old-fashioned sleigh bells, deerskin moccasins for ladies, antique lamps, linens of all kinds, an Austrian backscrubber "for joyful males and healthy females," pudding spoons, tea caddies, thermometers, food baskets, whiskbrooms, bayberry candles, and on and on and on! All of it crammed into a room about the size of a walk-in closet. Miss Anne or Miss Amy could reach under the counter and come up with something you never dreamed existed if you resisted all the things that were displayed. You didn't stand a chance of escaping them.

I stopped by to talk to the Quigley sisters. There was still a chance, in my mind, that the Duchess had, quite simply, mislaid Teddy somewhere in the inn. If a guest picked him up a logical place to turn him in might be the gift shop. They sold dolls and toys. As a matter of fact there were three teddy bears sitting on a high shelf.

Miss Anne and Miss Amy were standing behind the glassed-in counter for their bakery goods.

"Miss Walton has lost her teddy bear," I said. "It occurred to me someone might have turned it in here."

"Poor woman, she found the body, didn't she?" Miss Anne said.

"No dear, she *saw* the body from her window," Miss Amy said.

They always correct each other. They are both unnatural blondes, stylish stouts, ever smiling.

"No one has turned in Teddy," Miss Amy said.

"They would surely take it to the desk," Miss Anne said.

"Her good luck charm," Miss Amy said.

"More than that," Miss Anne said, in a stage whisper. "It was given to her by her *lover*!"

"Oh, my!" Miss Amy said.

"He was such a handsome man, even in his eighties!" Miss Anne said.

"Anne!" Miss Amy said, apparently shocked by that comment.

"If Teddy turns up here we'll let you know, Mr. Burton," Miss Anne said. "He was handsome—Mr. Krider, I mean."

"He's more likely to turn up at the desk," Miss Amy said. "Teddy, I mean."

I left them before they could turn to a sales pitch, apparently squabbling over the propriety of mentioning old scandals to a stranger. I'd only known them for fifteen years, and worked for the "lover."

In the lobby I told Chips about the missing bear.

"I've never known her to forget him or leave him lying around," Chips said. "I'll pass the word and keep an eye open for him."

"Folwell coming up empty?" I asked.

"He's down to the last half dozen," Chips said. "Drawn a blank so far."

"If I don't get an hour's nap I'm going to pass out on my feet," I said. "Give me a call if there's anything worth hearing about, will you, pal?"

I walked out the front door, across the lawn and the highway to my cottage. I know I'm not psychic, but I had that feeling of hackles rising again. Someone, I told myself, was watching me from the inn.

I opened the door and stepped in, calling out to the dog. I froze there. Old Jock was lying just inside the little foyer. There was a small gash on his forehead and around it some of the golden-grey fur was matted. He had been killed with something sharp and lethal. I didn't have to step past the poor old fellow to see that my house had been turned inside out, struck by a tornado.

I knelt beside Jocko and touched his still-warm body. He had tried to protect his new home and paid for it with his life. I began to swear, slowly, steadily, my voice rising until it became a shout of fury.

My first sense of outrage was connected to the fact that there were six police cars parked not fifty yards away on the grounds of the Red Cardinal. It was just about noon, broad daylight. I had only been away about an hour, after phoning Mark Stone in New York. In that time someone had come into the house, slugged poor old Jock who was at least sounding an alarm, and gone over my house. I was about to say "from top to bottom," but it is a ranch-style place, all on one level, with a big picture window looking out toward the hills. There's a nice big living room, a kitchen with a dining alcove, a small room which the real estate agent had called "a study" but which was really a large telephone booth with windows, and two bedrooms with a connecting bath. I took it as it came when I bought it, and I bought it because I had to be near the Duchess, and at the same time needed more privacy than the well-staffed inn could provide. The way it came was with very mod furniture, a lot of chrome and triangular tables. You were surprised when you sat down in a chair to find it comfortable despite its angles and curlicues. Not my taste, but well-fitted to my needs.

You couldn't sneak up on the place, for Pete's sake! It was right out in the open, on the main street of Camden.

My first thought, as I knelt beside the dead dog, was that this was the work of a psychotic Josh Krider, getting even for the lesson I'd taught him earlier that morning. But as I began to move around I wondered how sound a theory that was.

Nothing was broken, except a single coffee cup that had been on the kitchen sink drainboard, toppled over and snapped off its handle in the sink. I began to get a curious picture. Everything that could *hold* anything had been examined. In the kitchen, cups, cooking pots, two glass jars in which I kept sugar and flour had been emptied, contents scattered, an opened can of coffee dumped out in the same fashion. Nothing replaced, as if haste had been vital. The oven door, the ice box door stood open. Packages in the freezer compartment had been unwrapped, freezer foil scattered around the floor.

In the rest of the house every drawer in every table, bureau, and the desk in my study, had been pulled out and dumped. My clothes had been taken off the hangers in the bedroom closet, every pocket turned inside out. Whoever it was had examined every pair of shoes. But nothing had been wantonly destroyed or damaged, just searched and scattered. It seemed to me that Josh Krider, getting revenge, would have smashed things. Whoever was responsible for this had been looking for something that would fit in a coffee mug, the pocket of a suit or a pair of pants, the toe of a shoe.

In the old days, when I was guarding Wilfred Krider, I had worn a shoulder holster which contained a .44 caliber hand gun. The searcher had found this equipment in the study desk, taken the gun out of the holster, dropped them both on the floor and left them there. There was a box of cartridges, and these had been dumped out, as if what he was looking for could have been buried under them in the box.

I didn't touch anything except the gun and the holster. I strapped on the holster, fitted the gun into it, and put on a denim jacket. The days for going without a gun around this neighborhood were over.

I used a handkerchief to pick up the phone in the study, and dialed the Red Cardinal's number. I told the switchboard girl I needed Captain Folwell in a hurry.

It was Sergeant Lacey who came across the street from the inn. Either he was on his second tour of duty or he'd had a very long night. He had that cold-blue trooper look when I opened the door for him.

"What now?" he asked, as if I had deliberately done something to make things difficult for him.

I took him inside and pointed to Jock, lying in a pool of his own drying blood. Lacey looked, and then let his eyes drift around the area beyond.

"Holy Toledo!" he said.

"This has happened in the last hour and fifteen minutes," I said. "I came here around breakfast time, changed my clothes, drove up Camden Mountain to pay a visit to the Kriders. I came back here after a while, bringing the dog with me. He was an old friend from when I used to work up there. I made a phone call, and then went across to the inn. I hadn't gotten anything from the Kriders that would help Folwell. I wanted to report to him and come back here for a nap. Seems like I've been up for a month. But I got caught up in trying to find the Duchess's teddy bear."

"Doing *what?*"

"Somebody has 'kidnapped' the old lady's teddy bear—her good luck charm."

"Good lord," Lacey said, sounding disgusted.

"It's important to her, man," I said. "I talked to her, talked to the floor maid, to the Miss Quigleys who run the gift shop, passed the word to Chips about the missing bear, and came back here. I found this."

"Stuff smashed up!"

"Nothing is smashed up—except one coffee mug that fell off the sink. He was looking for something that would fit into a small place—a coffee cup, a suit coat pocket, a shoe."

Lacey gave me his cold look. "Drugs?" he suggested. The modern policeman's mind at work.

"Not here," I said.

"Then what?"

"I haven't the faintest idea. I don't have anything that I would hide. God himself would come looking for something here and my conscience would be clear. There just isn't—wasn't—anything to look for."

"Why would someone kill the dog?"

"Obviously Jock tried to interfere with him, or whoever it was thought he would try."

"I'd better get back to the Captain with this," Lacey said.

"And bring back your fingerprint genius with you," I said. "Whoever did this handled a lot of things—little things. He couldn't have been wearing mittens. I haven't touched anything but this." I opened my jacket and showed him the holster and gun.

"You got a license to carry that?" he asked.

"You know damn well I have."

"You think this may have some connection with what happened over at the inn?"

"If it doesn't," I said, "it's the biggest damn coincidence in the history of coincidences."

The troopers came and finally went, after powdering and dusting for prints and photographing every inch of the place. It took them a couple of hours, and I thought I was going to have to prop up my eyelids with match sticks to stay awake. I was that groggy. At last I was alone with Folwell. He's quite a different piece of goods from the Sergeant. Maybe he and Lacey played the old police game of the good guy and the bad guy; there's the one who treats you like a human being and protects you from the other one who bullies you. It's a standard routine in interrogations and it usually works with an innocent victim. I think Folwell knew that as an ex-cop I was too sophisticated to fall for that kind of game. In any event, he stayed behind when the others left to develop their fingerprint evidence and their pictures.

The fingerprint boys had picked up quite a few clear impressions on things. "What are they likely to find that we can account for?" Folwell asked. He was standing in the middle of the living room, looking around at the mess.

"Mine," I said, "on almost everything. There's a local woman who comes in once a week to do a thorough cleaning for me. She's due tomorrow, which means she hasn't been here for six days."

"People in and out?" he asked.

"I don't have much of a social life here," I said. "I do most of my drinking across the street. If I want to feed someone I take them out."

"Women?" he asked.

"Will you believe I've been a saint this past week? And speaking of drinking, it's a little early in the day but I could use a slug of something. How about you?"

He gave me a wry smile. "Technically, I've just gone off duty," he said.

I went into the kitchen, poured two stiff Jack Daniels on the rocks, and brought them back. Folwell was sitting in one of my crazy-shaped modern chairs. We toasted each other silently and drank.

"This whole mess doesn't make any sense," he said. He waved around at the room. "I don't mean this. Lacey reports you think there's some connection between this and the murder at the inn." He raised a questioning eyebrow at me. He was a tired man, he needed a shave, he needed to go somewhere and soak his head—like me.

"Our Mr. X was looking for something in the old lady's room," I said. "He didn't find it, or he didn't have time to look before she caught him there. Her history? Over forty years the mistress of Wilfred Krider. My history, ten years the bodyguard of Wilfred Krider and five years looking out for the old lady. Ten years ago a head-on encounter with Mr. X."

"But Mr. X isn't responsible for what happened here," Folwell said, frowning. "He's been dead since Monday."

"Ten years ago he had an ally, an accomplice, who got him away after I'd shot him. That ally could have gotten back in the act."

Folwell took another long swallow of his drink. "Let me tell you some things that have happened in the last twelve hours," he said. He glanced at his watch. "It's just about twelve hours now since the old lady spotted Mr. X in the pool."

"It feels like a month," I said.

He nodded. "First thing we did was take the finger prints off the body. His prints—taken by us. A preliminary check with the state police files in Hartford, with the FBI in Washington, with the CIA—nothing. No record of those prints. Now our Mr. X had to be in his middle or late forties, I'd guess. Not many adult males have gone un-fingerprinted in this country—for security reasons, in the Services, because he's committed a crime. Mr. X has no record—so far."

"Our bad luck," I said.

"Maybe it's not luck. There are some kinds of people whose records get eliminated, removed from the files," Folwell said. "People working in national security of some kind, CIA agents, for example. They work under a false identity, and if they get caught or killed, no one can trace who they are. There are people who work for the big multi-national corporations, security jobs, whose identities are wiped out in some fashion."

"Krider Industries!" I said.

"Could be," Folwell said. "They are big enough, powerful enough to have faceless, recordless guys working for them."

"But Mr. X was trying to kill the head man ten years ago," I said.

"Maybe someone in K.I. was trying to get to be the head man," Folwell said. He was no dummy, this state trooper captain. I had thought that same thought quite a few times. Mr. X, a hit-man for Mark Stone ten years ago. That was how he'd gotten through the gates, past the electric fence, almost into the house. Mark Stone's other men had looked the other way.

"So you keep coming up Krider," I said.

Folwell drained his glass and put it down on the table beside his chair. "I don't know why I have an inclination to trust you, Dan," he said. "When we first met up with Mr. X, everyone connected with the Kriders seemed to be talking out of both corners of their mouths at once. Including the Old Man himself. You told me a straight story then, and nothing ever turned up to make me doubt it. You don't honestly know what someone could have been looking for here?"

"So help me," I said.

"The Old Man never gave you anything to keep for him?"

"Not anything I would keep in a shoe," I said. "He left me the responsibility of looking out for the Duchess. There have never been any problems until last night—and today." I laughed. "Today, when she claims her teddy bear was kidnapped."

He stood up to go. "I didn't tell you, did I, that we found the bear?"

"Where? She'll be glad to get it back."

"One of the kitchen helpers found it in the trash after Chips had spread the word. I doubt, however, that Miss Walton will be glad to see him the way he is."

"What do you mean?"

Folwell gave me a steady look. "The bear was cut open, all the stuffing taken out of him."

"For Pete's sake, why?" I said.

Folwell shrugged. "Anything that would fit into a coffee cup, or the toe of a shoe, would fit into that teddy bear's insides," he said. "Microfilm? Some kind of mathematical formula?"

Part Two

One

I remember reading a detective story when I was a kid, by G. K. Chesterton I think it was, which propounded a truth that I've never forgotten as a cop. "Where do you hide a leaf? In a forest." A guy robs a bank and gets caught running down an alley, he's had it. If he gets caught running through Grand Central Station he's catching a train!

Captain Folwell, I knew, was champing at the bit to get into action. He had a murder, malicious mischief and theft in the case of the ripped-open teddy bear, and breaking and entering, criminal mischief, and the death of a dog at my place. Who to look for and where? I gave him the Chesterton line.

"In a forest—where there are people," I said. "All the bastard has to do is sit around the lobby of the Red Cardinal, or watch the color TV set in the TV room; or go about his job there if that's his cover. To disappear would give him away."

Folwell nodded. We were in Dick Carson's office behind the lobby in the Red Cardinal. It's a dark little room illuminated by a strip of fluorescent light in the ceiling. I don't think Dick uses it for much except as a place to retreat when he needs privacy, or to make an unoverheard phone call. He has a private line in there that doesn't go through the switchboard.

"Who he is keeps eating at me," Dick said. He looked almost as pooped as Folwell and I did. "Is he the guy who helped Mr. X escape from *Hilltop* ten years ago? Has he been living here in Camden all that time, waiting for another call to action? Can he have been here for ten years working in my hotel?"

"How many ten-year veterans have you got?" Folwell asked.

Dick ticked them off on his fingers. "Chips, Fritz Schlee, my head cook, Mrs. Kramer, the baker, Dominic, the short order cook, Grover Jones and Tom Bently, my two outdoor men, Dave Palmer, my head bartender, my aunts, the Quigley sisters in the gift shop, Rose Garner at the front desk, Mildred, the second-floor maid." He gave us a twisted smile. "And of course there's the Duchess who's lived in those second-floor rooms since before I took over twenty years ago."

"Other help changes from year to year?" Folwell asked.

"Some have been here two, three, four years. Young girl waitresses become local housewives, or take off to where they think the lights are brighter. Temporary kitchen help—they move on because they don't see any long-term future in the work. Most of them are locals, eager to get out of a small town as they get older."

"Have people who worked for Krider Industries stayed here in the past when they came to see Mr. Krider?"

Dick shook his head. "I thought that was going to be a source of income when I took over, quite a few rooms a year. Would you believe that if there ever were any they never stayed at the Red Cardinal? I think Krider didn't want anyone connected with his business to notice his visits to the lady on the second floor. When they came here I think he put them up at the Pine Tree in Lakesburg, or the Covered Bridge Inn over in Silver Springs—places like that. I never got to see them or know them."

"And yet this whole thing smells of Krider," Folwell said. "Krider owned this inn before he passed it on to you, right? Miss Walton was his woman, right? Her room is searched. Her good luck bear is stolen, ripped up."

"Not by the same guy who searched her room," I said. "He

was two days dead when Teddy disappeared."

"It still smells of Krider," Folwell said. "They don't find what they want in the lady's rooms, or in her toy. So where do they go next? To Krider's ex-bodyguard and security man, right?" He brought his fist down on Dick's desk. "When you've got nothing to work with you have to rely on guesses. I'm guessing someone thinks Wilfred Krider left something in the care of someone he trusted. First they try you, someone Krider cared enough about to leave him a chunk of money and the care of his beloved Miss Walton. So what the hell is it he left in trusted hands?"

"No idea. Not in my hands. Miss Walton says, 'nothing.'"

Folwell gave me a hard look. "Krider's world is a world of sinister secrets, obscure maneuverings, bloody violence when necessary. If he asked you to keep a secret you'd keep it, wouldn't you, Dan?"

"Yes," I said. "But he didn't ask me to keep a secret, Captain. Nor did he ask me to hide something that might contain a secret. He had a theory. What I didn't know I couldn't be forced to tell. I think he dealt with the Duchess the same way. Neither one of us were in on his business shenanigans."

"Meanwhile the murderer of Mr. X is sniffing around my hotel," Dick Carson said. "If we don't catch up with him I won't have ten customers here over the weekend. The story's already on the radio and TV."

"Oh, I don't know," Folwell said. "People love to be in the center of excitement when it's over. I bet you'll be crowded."

"But is it over?" I asked him.

The Captain didn't look fond of me.

The local veterinary cremated Jock for me. Have I mentioned that we never found what had been used to brain the old fellow? It hadn't been the poker out of my fireplace set, or anything else I kept in the foyer or the hall closet. Old Jock's killer must have been carrying some kind of weapon when the dog blocked him. I wondered, sourly, if the weapon, whatever it had been, was meant to use on me in case I showed up when the search was under way. Jock had been unexpected, if the searcher knew my habits. He'd been a part of my establishment for less than an hour when he was hit.

It was about four o'clock in the afternoon when I got back from the vet's and Jock's cremation. I was so tired that my joints ached. Under normal conditions I'd have taken a steaming hot shower, crawled in between the sheets, and slept it out. But conditions weren't normal. I didn't bother to straighten up any of the mess. I lay down on top of my bed, fully clothed. An old habit, almost forgotten, reasserted itself. I found myself loosening my .44 in its holster, to make certain it would slide out easily if I needed it. I closed my eyes, but sleep didn't come.

You'd have to have lived my kind of life to understand why tensions didn't relax. Someone had searched my house, looking for something that wasn't there to find. I'd suffered no loss, except the broken handle on one coffee mug. You'd probably say it was over. Whoever it was wouldn't come back. I didn't have what he wanted. He'd dealt with me, and he'd dealt with the Duchess. We could forget about him.

My mind didn't work that way. Every instinct I had told me that it wasn't over; that it could be just beginning. The man who had stolen Teddy and ripped him open to find some small object, who had turned my place upside-down searching for that same small object, had to make his next move. If that "small object" was so important to him, he would. He was capable of violence to get what he wanted. Mr. X was in the police morgue with a hole in his head; Old Jock was ashes in the vet's crematory.

Wilfred Krider had indoctrinated me very thoroughly in the techniques of terror. Men in other parts of the world—or perhaps just down the street—were being subjected to inhuman torture to pry information from them. We live in a world where information is the key to survival; information in sophisticated computers, information in men's minds. The Duchess insisted she didn't have any information about Wilfred's operations; I didn't have any. That didn't mean that the man who assumed we had such information wouldn't resort to violence now to dig out of us what he thought we had.

I remember Krider said to me once. "Don't ever brush aside the possibilities of violence, Daniel. You only have to look around to know that we're living in an age of lurid public melodrama. Laugh it off and you'll get burned to the bone."

And so I didn't, couldn't, sleep. The chances were that with the troopers alerted the man who was after what he thought I had wouldn't come again in broad daylight. Too many people were on the lookout for any kind of strange moves.

"Sleep, you dummy!" I told myself. It wouldn't happen.

Then someone was beating on my front door with the brass knocker.

He wouldn't come that way, warning me of his arrival, I thought. Yet he could be a friend, an acquaintance, someone I would let in without a second thought; Chips, Dick Carson, someone from the inn with a message. Judas Priest, I was getting so I would suspect my own father.

I opened the door, one hand slipped inside my jacket and on the butt of my .44. I was surprised. Standing there was Laura Stark. She was wearing jeans and a T-shirt. She looked sweet, she smelled wonderful.

"Wondered about you, Dan," she said. "If you're napping, forget it."

I don't often use the word "beautiful" for a woman. To me beauty lies in personality, not bone structure. Laura does have bone structure, though; high cheek bones, a wide mouth, generous, relaxed; candid blue eyes that asked for honesty; slim, but with graceful curves; reddish blonde hair worn shoulder length. You might look at her a second time if you saw her across that crowded room. Once you talked to her for awhile you didn't want her to go anywhere.

I held the door open for her. "Come on in," I said. "I *was* lying down, but it doesn't seem to get me anywhere."

She stepped through the foyer and into my upside-down living room.

"My heavens!" she said. "They told me over at the inn that someone had . . . " She gestured at the disorder.

"He didn't find what he was looking for because I don't have anything to find," I said. "Coffee, tea, coke?"

"They said something about a dog. I didn't know you had a dog."

"I didn't, until this morning." I told her about Jock and how he'd happened to be in the house.

"How awful," she said. "You don't have any idea who—?"

"None."

"Or why?"

I told her the notion that someone had been looking for a small object that would fit into a coffee mug, a shoe, a toy bear. I sketched in the possible connection with the Kriders.

She listened, a small frown furrowing her smooth, white forehead. There was something so innocent and vulnerable about this girl—like a baby chick, sort of soft, fragile, light. I kept holding back with her—wondering what she'd see in a tough old bird like me, but I'd had fantasies about her. Oh yes, I had fantasies. Never thought I'd sit around mooning over a dame, but there I'd been all summer, hanging around that piano, listening to this little music major, just graduated from Vassar, with all her big dreams about writing music for Broadway shows—I just let her ramble on. Let her have her dreams—she was doing so much for mine. Besides, some of her songs weren't bad at all.

She didn't ask any more questions. "You're exhausted," she said.

"Like thirty-six hours without sleep," I said. "Trouble is, whenever I close my eyes I think I hear footsteps in the back hall."

"Try to sleep, Dan," she said. "I'll stay here and answer your phone, or the door if someone comes calling. I don't have to report for work till ten o'clock. That'll give you five hours."

"Now, you don't honestly think I can go to sleep with you sitting here, do you, doll?" I said.

She smiled, but I could see I'd made her uncomfortable. She walked around the room, looking at the mess, and stopped at my bedroom door.

"Really, Dan," she said earnestly, "I mean it. You've got to get some sleep." I felt absurdly pleased at her concern. "C'mon and lie down on the bed," she urged, "and I'll stand guard."

I walked over to her and looked into those steady blue eyes. I took her face in my hands and planted a kiss on her forehead. Now was not the time for anything else. "You are an incredible love," I murmured. "You really do mean it, don't you."

"I certainly do," she said firmly. "Now take off your jacket and lie down. I'll keep the bogey-man away."

"Yes, ma'm. Only too happy to." I took off my jacket and I heard her sharp intake of breath. She was staring at my shoulder holster and the .44 handgun.

"What every well-dressed gunman wears," I said.

"You, Dan?"

"I haven't worn it for a long time," I said. "Not since Wilfred Krider died. I was his bodyguard, you know."

"I didn't know."

I stretched out on the bed and felt my eyelids drooping immediately. "Oh, man . . . I'm so tired." I mumbled. "You're an angel of mercy, Laura . . . you don't have to stay . . . "

She sat on the edge of the bed and her cool fingers stroked my cheek. "I'll be here when you wake up," she said softly.

Sleep was creeping up on me at last, and just before I slipped off, I remember thinking maybe she really cares for me . . . she must really care about me.

It wasn't what you would call "pitch dark" when I came up out of that deep well of sleep. The moon that had stared down at Mr. X in the swimming pool gave the night a pale blue look, and a galaxy of lights from the windows of the Red Cardinal and from the outside lighting fixtures gave the whole area the visibility of a ball park prepared for a night game.

But there were no lights in my cottage. The bedroom door was open and the rooms beyond were without light. For a moment or so I wasn't quite oriented. I reached out and turned on the bedside lamp. I glanced at my watch. It was 11:30.

Laura? She was gone, of course. She went on in the lounge at ten o'clock. She must not have had the heart to wake me when she had to go.

I stretched and sat up. I felt good. A little more than seven hours' sleep had worked its magic. I switched on lights, stripped, and had myself a good hot shower. I put on a clean turtleneck and a beige gabardine suit that Laura had also noticed—that girl had an eye for men's clothes. Before I put on the coat, however, I strapped on the holster with the .44 in place.

Outside the cottage I could hear the voices of people still gathered around the pool. It was a hot night, like the night before. People took their drinks out there on a night like this. The doors were open to the lounge but I didn't hear the piano. Of course she took breaks from time to time.

I crossed the lawn and went around the corner of the inn to the pool. There were perhaps a dozen or fifteen people sitting at tables on the terrace. I could tell, from the sound of voices, that the lounge was crowded.

I wanted to check in with Laura, but I decided that first I'd better see how the Duchess was doing. I hadn't seen her since they'd told her about Teddy. She must have felt neglected.

I ducked in a side door to the lobby and looked into the TV room. Chips was there, looking at something on the TV set, which seemed to run twenty-four hours a day.

"If you're headed for the Duchess," he said, "she's in the lounge."

"She took the news about Teddy in stride?"

Chips grinned. "Center of attraction. Discovered a dead man last night, her good luck charm stolen and hacked up by the killer. Queen of the May." He looked me over. "I take it you got some rest."

"Yes. Thanks to Laura."

His eyes widened behind his horn-rimmed glasses. "How do you mean?"

"She offered to sit around and keep an eye on things while I got some shuteye. Would you believe, I couldn't relax without someone holding the fort?"

"Is Laura over at your place now?" Chips asked.

"Of course not. She's here—isn't she?"

"Never showed up for work," Chips said. "Dick's burned up at her. Good crowd and suddenly he has no entertainment in the lounge. Didn't even call him to say she wasn't coming in."

I felt a little shiver run along my spine. "She promised to stay in my place till I woke up—or until she had to go to work at ten."

"So what happened?"

"Nothing happened!" We stood there looking at each other like a couple of quiz kids confronted with questions they couldn't answer. "I woke up at eleven thirty. She was gone. I supposed I'd been sleeping so soundly she didn't want to wake me—came back here to do her job."

"Well, she didn't come, and she didn't let Dick know why," Chips said.

Two

Chips and I must have been wondering the same thing.

"I'll check her room again." he said, and took off.

Laura had been assigned a little room that was tucked away over the kitchen where she could work at the piano without bothering any guests. Dick had moved in a little spinet piano for her to use during her engagement for the season.

Chips had a passkey, and I followed him into the room. It all looked perfectly normal, bed neatly made, some sheets of ruled music paper on the little piano, clothes on hangers in the closet. I was conscious of the faint scent of the perfume she wore. Chips and I looked at each other.

"It doesn't look as if she came back here," he said. He was fingering the clothes in the closet. "The things she wears on the job are all here."

"Maybe she bought something new," I said, a weak attempt not to face facts. She had intended to go to work. She had intended to wake me before she left my house. She hadn't done either thing.

"It doesn't *have* to be anything bad," Chips said, looking vaguely around the little room.

"Think of something good," I said.

He couldn't, and neither could I. Of course it didn't *have* to be related to the horrors we'd been involved in for the last day. You ever waited for a girl who's late for a date? You begin to assume she's been raped, or run over by a truck. It turns out she encountered an old school friend and stopped somewhere for a drink or a chat. "I had no way to reach you," she explains. In my house, Laura had been less than fifty yards away from where she lived and worked. There were phones all over the place. If she were all right there was no possible explanation for her not letting someone know why she wasn't going to report for work.

"She has a car, doesn't she?" I asked Chips.

"Little Chevette hatchback," he said. "It's out there in the parking lot. I noticed when we came over here."

"I thought perhaps she forgot something in town she had to have," I said. "Makeup from the drug store, headache pills—something."

"The drug store is half a mile away," Chips said. "It closes at eight o'clock. It is now midnight."

"I was thinking of a car accident. No I.D., so no one here notified," I said.

"Stop playing games," Chips said. "Her car is there in the parking lot so she didn't wreck it. If she was hitching a ride from someone and they wrecked up badly enough to keep Laura from contacting us for hours, then the call for an ambulance would come to the Red Cardinal's switchboard. Part of our service to the community. We take all calls for the volunteer fire department, volunteer ambulance service—call the right people. We'd be the first to know. There's been no accident."

We switched off the lights in Laura's room and stepped out into the moonlight. My mother would have said it was "a night for lovers," pale, soft, warm. Unless we could come up with the answer to Laura's unexplained absence there was nothing romantic about the evening.

"When did she come over to your place?" Chips asked.

"About four-thirty," I said. "I lay down on my bed a few minutes after four to try for a nap. Nothing doing. Then she knocked on the door. She volunteered to stick around so I could relax and get some shut-eye. I was grateful. The last thing she said to me was 'I'll be here when you wake up.'"

"But she wasn't."

"No. It was about 11:30 when I woke. She'd mentioned that she had to be at work at ten. I was sleeping so solidly I figured she just decided to let me have it out. I don't think she thought I was in any danger. I don't think I was, really."

"But you don't know if she left at five, or six, or eight, or ten?"

"I was out like a light," I said. "Maybe she remembered something she had to do."

"More important than turning up for her job—without phoning Dick to explain?"

"It's not like her."

"You're damn right it's not," Chips said. "Look, you explain to Dick what's happened. I'll call the state police."

Those were the words—state police—that neither of us had wanted to speak. We'd run out of non-sinister explanations for what had happened to Laura.

I went back into the lounge and stood looking around at the customers. Dave Palmer, the regular bartender, was behind the stick. He's one of Dick's old hands, bald as an egg, with a wry sense of humor that delighted the regular customers. He spotted me and waved. The room was noisy, a drinking crowd enjoying themselves. Most of the people there I knew by sight, including the two young men, Spencer and Wallace, who were in Camden for a golf tournament, and, somewhat surprisingly, Mr. and Mrs. Townsend, who had said they were just passing through on the way to a vacation spot further north. Evidently the excitement at the Red Cardinal had decided them against moving on right away.

In a far corner of the oak-panelled room, the Duchess sat in her regular booth. Dick Carson was with her, looking relaxed in spite of his troubles. Half a dozen of the local young people were grouped around. It wasn't unusual. The Duchess, when she was in the mood, could be fascinating with her nostalgic memories of Broadway fifty years ago, of the West

End theaters in London after World War I, in Paris, in Berlin. Tonight, I suspected, she was at the center of something much more luridly current—a dead man in the pool outside, a hacked-up toy. There was, I thought bitterly, quite a lot she didn't know about yet.

After a bit I caught Dick Carson's attention and beckoned to him. He excused himself and came over to the corner of the bar where I was standing. I brought him up to date on Laura, not why she wasn't here doing her thing because I had no idea why she wasn't.

"She didn't leave you a note or anything?"

I hadn't looked, because when I left my house I'd had no reason to think she'd done anything but go to work. She hadn't left a note in any obvious place where I was bound to see it. It could, I supposed, have blown off onto the floor from where she'd left it and I hadn't looked.

In the next hour there was a great deal of activity without any results. There was no note in my house. A Sergeant Belter responded to Chips' call to the state police. He was able to assure us that there'd been no reports of any kind of accidents. In daylight saving time, it doesn't get dark until nearly eight-thirty at that time in the summer. A guest of the inn, a middle-aged traveling lady, had been sitting under one of the colored umbrellas on the inn's lawn about four in the afternoon and she had seen Laura go to my house. She knew her from having heard her play in the lounge the night before. She didn't see Laura come out and she'd remained under the umbrella till well after five o'clock. Sergeant Belter wasn't able to locate anyone else who had seen Laura go to the cottage or leave it.

Belter followed the normal police approach. How did she happen to be here? Dick Carson had been in Poughkeepsie on business a couple of months ago. He had stopped for lunch at an inn there and heard a young Vassar graduate playing piano. He was intrigued by her kind of music and hired her for the summer through Labor Day for the Red Cardinal's lounge. She'd been in Camden since early July, a popular acquisition.

Of course she'd met a lot of people in those four weeks.

"Men?" Belter asked.

"She's an attractive kid," Dick said. "It would be unnatural if our male customers hadn't paid her special attention."

Which brought Belter around to me, naturally enough.

"You were more than just a music lover," he said.

"I hoped to be," I said.

"She was going to baby-sit while you got some sleep?"

"You know about what happened in my cottage earlier?"

"Yes. So she was going to guard you. From what?"

"Wake me if there was a return visit," I said.

"So that's being friends," he said.

"Look, I'll give it to you on the line," I said. We were in Dick's office with only Dick as audience. "I had a thing for her, I admit—but she's just a kid! Listen, I was afraid of her—she's the kind that makes a guy do crazy things. Like wanting to get married, for Pete's sake! Anyway, I didn't want to rush her into anything—yet. I was trying to be patient."

"So you decided not to be patient and she walked out on you—or tried to walk out on you," he suggested.

"Okay, okay . . . you've got to ask questions." I was only a little angry. He was a cop. I would have asked the same kind of questions if it had been my case. "We've had a few after-hours drinks together—took a couple of bike rides around the countryside. But she really worked hard on her music compositions. I don't think she was giving time to any other men around." I was interested to know if that were true.

"She got along well with staff people," Dick Carson told the trooper. "She is outgoing, but private, is the way I'd describe her. She recognized me and Chips as people who could help her if she had any problems—with guests, with routines. My aunts,the Quigley sisters in the gift shop, took a shine to her. I think she had dinner with them at their home a couple of times. The Duchess enjoyed her playing, invited her up to her rooms to show her the picture gallery—old-time matinee idols who had been her friends. Beyond that, I don't think Laura was social with anyone. Of course people crowded around her when she was playing, flattered her, probably invited her to do things. But she concentrated on her composing in the daytime and her work at night." He smiled at me. "Dan is the only person I thought was really hanging in there."

There are two phones on the desk in Dick's office, one his private line, the other connected to the inn's switchboard. The switchboard phone rang and Dick answered it.

"Yes, he's here," Dick said. "For you, Dan."

For just a moment I thought it might be Laura with an explanation.

"Dan Burton here," I said.

It wasn't Laura. A colorless male voice responded.

"I think you know what we were looking for in your house, Burton."

"Who is this?" I made wild signals to Dick to have someone listen in on the call. The switchboard was only a few steps down the hall outside his office. He took off.

"If you care at all about seeing the girl alive again and in one piece," the voice said, "You will produce what we want."

"You have Miss Stark?" I asked. I could feel a cold knot forming in my gut.

"The fact that I know she's missing should answer that question," the voice said.

"I don't know what you want. How can I produce it if I don't know what it is?" My voice wasn't steady.

"I think you know what it is," I was told. "I know the old lady knows what it is. Between you, get it. It will be too awkward to hang onto Miss Stark very long."

"If Miss Walton knows what it is, how do I get in touch with you."

"We'll call you one hour after the banks open in the morning. And we'll only call you that once, Burton."

The phone went dead.

So it was a kidnapping. Dick came back from the switchboard. They had a recorder out there, used to take ambulance or fire calls. He was able to play back the last of the conversation to Belter.

"You recognize the voice?" Belter asked.

"No."

"What is it they want."

"I don't have the remotest idea," I said.

"This is for Captain Folwell," Belter said. "It's obviously part of his case."

Dick and I made tracks for the bar and the Duchess. She was still holding court there, telling about a date she had once had with John Barrymore. She was reluctant to leave, but Dick and I managed to persuade her that it was something important about the late Mr. X.

It took her a few minutes to get her strength organized to make the retreat to the second floor and her apartment.

"Nice kids," she said, when we were in her jumble room. "I hated to leave them. You know I don't know anything about the dead man beyond what I've reported."

I told her, quickly, about Laura and the phone call. She sank down into what Dick calls her throne—a high-backed arm chair. The color had faded from her face, leaving only the spots of rouge on her high cheek bones.

"If you know what it is they're after, Duchess, tell me," I said. "Laura's safety may depend on it."

She just sat there, staring at us.

"This guy on the phone mentioned banks," Dick said. "Do either of you have safety deposit boxes anywhere? He seemed to think you might be keeping what he wants in a bank."

I, for sure, didn't have a safety deposit box anywhere. I

kept my rather handsome inheritance from the Old Man in a savings account and a modest checking account in the Camden Bank. No deposit box.

The Duchess had been left a million bucks, and probably a lot more jewelry than what was scattered on her dressing table.

"I have an account in the Manhattan Trust in New York," she said, finally. "There is a safety deposit box, but there is nothing in it."

"Nothing—?"

"Will Krider thought I should have some place to keep my jewelry safe," she said. "He rented a box for me at Manhattan Trust, and because Will thought I didn't have a head for business, it was rented for the rest of my life, to be paid for automatically out of my account. A nice young man named Willingham takes care of it for me."

"Why rent a safety deposit if you don't use it?" Dick asked her.

"Because Will fixed it that way," she said. "I never understood the use of owning beautiful jewels if you couldn't wear them, had to keep them locked away. I suppose some people buy them simply as an investment. Will bought them to please me." She smiled at us as though she'd just delivered the Sermon on the Mount.

Screw Wilfred Krider's romantic notions! I had known him well for ten years and he was about as romantic as a man-eating shark—except, perhaps, in his approach to Martha Walton. He certainly hadn't bought jewelry as an investment. The money involved had hurt him no more than it would have hurt me to buy glass beads for some chick. He had simply wanted to decorate his sex object. Looking at the Duchess now it was hard to think of her that way. But there was that painting in the next room!

There was also Laura in the hands of some psycho. The voice on the phone had been so certain that the Duchess and I knew what he wanted, presumably something that, if it weren't lying around in my shoe or the Duchess's teddy bear, could be in a safety deposit box somewhere, a box that belonged to one of us.

The Duchess seemed to have faded away from us, as if she had drifted back into that past she cherished. I tried to bring her back to now.

"Let me lay it out for you, luv," I said to the old woman. I bent over her, letting my hand rest gently on her shoulder. She looked up at me, responding to the touch, and I thought I could read fear in her wide, still clear, eyes. "This has to be a Krider game. I have his stamp on me and so do you. These people who have taken Laura thinks one of us knows where something that is important to them is. I swear to you, Duchess, that I have nothing, don't know about anything. It is some sort of object that could fit into a coffee cup, the toe of a shoe, inside Teddy. Captain Folwell suggested a microfilm, maybe a formula of some kind."

"Poor Teddy," she said, her eyes turned away. I guessed she was thinking back to the night when Wilfred Krider had given her the toy for good luck, and she had gone out on stage and knocked Broadway on its collective ears. It was only yesterday to her. I had to get her back to tonight.

"If anyone knows what they're after it has to be you, dear," I said.

She didn't speak for a moment. "Will they really harm the girl if we can't guess what it is?" she asked, finally.

"Guesses are all we've got," I said. "You want to hear some? Let's go back to Monday morning. The man we call Mr. X manages to get into your room while you're out for your morning walk. I have to guess he was looking for this small object that would fit into a coffee cup. Maybe he found it, because if he didn't and it's so important, why didn't he try to force you to turn it over to him? So somebody shoots him, thinking he has it. If he had it he must have been able to dispose of it before they caught up with him. They kill him, they hide his body, they try to check back on what he'd done with what they want so badly."

"Two sets of thieves?" Dick asked, sounding surprised.

"That's the way the pieces fit for me," I said. "After two days this second group decide Mr. X hadn't found what they wanted. Why dump his body in the pool, at some risk? I think it was meant to warn you, Duchess, or me, or someone else I haven't thought of, that that's how they'd deal with us if we held out on them. They probably searched your room again, stole Teddy, cut him open to find this—this object. No dice. Then, while I was out of my cottage, they went there, killed old Jock who tried to interfere, and took the place apart. They didn't find anything because there wasn't anything there. They must have stayed close by, watching. What would I do when I discovered the damage? The cops came, the place was photographed and fingerprinted. And I? I went to bed, watched over by a girl."

"And they—they came and took her?" the Duchess asked, her voice grown small and husky.

"How could I be thinking if I were playing their game?" I said. "They seem convinced that you or I have what they want. They have thought, at first, that one of us would keep whatever it is close to us. They have searched thoroughly, totally, and come up empty. There are thousands of acres of countryside around us. Something that would fit into a coffee cup could be hidden under rock in the woods and an army could search for it for the rest of this century and not find it. So they have to get at us some other way, and Laura is it." The old woman didn't speak, and I went on. "You ask me to guess if they will harm Laura if we don't come through for them. My guess is that they will."

"But we haven't got what they want!" the Duchess protested.

"I haven't got what they want," I said. "But think, Duchess, think! If Krider gave you something to hold for him—without telling you what its importance was—that had to be at least five years ago. It could have been twenty-five years ago! It could have been fifty years ago—put away somewhere, not thought of for all that time. Think—try to remember—try to recall."

Again she gave me that fear-tainted, wide-eyed look. "There isn't a single detail of my life with Will Krider that I've forgotten," she said. "Daniel, if I knew what they were talking about would I let them hurt that child?"

"Well, would you?" I asked.

She turned away, staring into the past again. Maybe if I let her up for a bit something would surface. Maybe she didn't have the instant recall about the Old Man she thought she had. *"Put this away for me somewhere, Martha,"* he says to her, maybe decades ago. She puts it away and since it's never mentioned again she forgets about it.

I wanted a drink and I knew where she kept her brandy in the kitchenette. Dick Carson followed me out there.

"She's so proud of her mental sharpness," he said. "She'll never admit to forgetting something."

I poured myself a slug of Hennessey and drank it. "It could be," I said, "that there is nothing to forget, that the man on the phone has guessed wrong."

"How did they get Laura out of your house?" Dick asked, shaking his head. "You were there asleep, but with a gun strapped on. All she had to do was cry out and you'd have been in action. I know you, Dan. I know how quickly you can react."

"I've wondered about that," I said. "Let's try a suppose. I'm asleep, but she's wide awake—sitting in my living room. Someone comes to the window, someone she knows." I smiled at him. "Could have been you, Chips, one of your aunt Quigleys. Whoever it is beckons to her to come outside. They don't want to wake me, she thinks. She goes outside and that's that. A gun in her ribs, a gag over her mouth."

Dick was staring at me. "Are you suggesting that I—?"

"I said let's suppose," I said. "But I'm surer than ever of one thing, Dick. A murder on Monday, a body hidden close by for two days and then dumped in the pool, a second search of these rooms, a search of my house in broad daylight, a return to my house to kidnap Laura. Somebody has been moving around here freely, not a stranger. It has to be a member of your staff, a guest, a regular customer. Someone whose presence here in the Red Cardinal is perfectly normal."

"Judas Priest!" he said.

"We've got until after the banks open tomorrow—say ten o'clock," I said. I glanced at my watch. "Nine hours. After that, who knows? Laura may also turn up in the pool."

Nine hours, most of them in the middle of the night, is no time at all when you have no real lead to follow. I could stay with the Duchess and try to prod her memory. I had been pretty close to the old girl for the last five years and I had to admit that I'd seen no signs of approaching senility. If anyone had questioned her mental faculties a few hours ago I'd have defended her to the limit. I knew what was happening to me. I wanted to think there was something she could remember if she tried, because I didn't know where else to look for answers.

Dick Carson had left the old lady's jumble room and gone back downstairs. I guess I'd given him something to think about, but there wasn't any handle on it. Where did he start looking in the Red Cardinal for a murderer and a kidnapper with a familiar, probably friendly, face? Nine hours in the middle of the night to follow perhaps fifty leads!

"Would you mind getting me a brandy, Daniel?" the Duchess asked, after Dick had said goodnight and left.

I knew her habits; two ounces of Hennessey on an ice cube in a little brandy snifter. When I brought it back from the kitchenette she was struggling to get a cigarette lighted. Her old hands weren't steady and she couldn't get her lighter to work. I held it for her and she drew smoke deep into her lungs, which was followed by a rasping cough. A couple of packs a day for seventy-five years she told me once. *"One of the few pleasures I have left these days, Daniel, and my lungs and I intend to outlast the danger to my health."* When she was a kid it was a scandalous thing for women to smoke in public. Only actresses and whores, synonymous to a lot of people, indulged in the habit. World War I had put an end to that ban at the same time that it had shut off the sale of legal liquor and made the bootlegger the hero-villain of the day. The Duchess had lived through all that, been a hit on Broadway, and then, as the big depression lowered the boom on the American economy in '29, she had fallen into the arms of Wilfred Krider. She had lived through recession, recovery, Franklin D. Roosevelt, Truman, Korea, Eisenhower, the murder of John F. Kennedy, Vietnam, Richard Nixon. It was a turgid history in which the man who kept her, loved her, lay beside her in her great bed under her nude portrait, was always very near the center of all the important action in those years. Krider Industries thrived in depression times and in boom times; they made huge profits off wars and there were always wars, major and minor; political changes required astute maneuvering, sometimes violence, and from what I know Wilfred Krider, at the helm of Krider Industries' golden ship, never steered a wrong course for his associates and stockholders. The fates of nations had been in his control, or at least heavily dependent on his reactions to situations, while he lay in the next room, in this quiet country inn, sharing what he chose to share with *the* woman in his life.

In all the turmoil surrounding this lifetime of love, the wars, the holocaust of the Nazi gas ovens, assassinations, murder in high places, political scandals, was it unreasonable that Martha Walton might have forgotten a casual request from her man. *"Hang onto this for me, Martha?"* No more than that perhaps. She didn't ask him questions about his business world, his family life. He told her what he wanted her to know, and she didn't ask him about anything else. I knew those were the Old Man's rules. The thing he gave her—which would fit into a coffee cup or the toe of a shoe—could have been a present for a grandchild, something for a business associate. It could have happened years and years ago. Perhaps they had unexpectedly gone on one of their trips to Europe, to the ends of the earth. She thinks of clothes, and luggage, and jewelry, and stockings, and perfume, and face creams, and hats, and shoes, and a visit to the hairdresser. He never mentions the thing he has given her to keep and the whole incident simply dissolves in the back of her mind.

That's the way I hoped it was, and that in the next nine hours I could, somehow, stimulate her capacity to recall this ancient history.

"I think I must go to bed, Daniel," she said. "This day has taken more out of me than I'm equipped to give."

I felt a little angry—and helpless. Laura's safety might depend on her, and yet, as I looked at her, I knew she was close to exhaustion. At ninety-four there were no reserves she could call on.

"Talk to me for just a few minutes more, dear," I said.

Her eyelids closed. "Please, Daniel—a little later," she said.

"There's so little time to get hooked into something," I said. "Try to answer one or two questions."

She didn't speak. She just sat there on her "throne," her tinted eyelids lowered. I wondered for an instant if she had quietly gone away. Her cigarette burned out in the ashtray beside her. She'd only taken half her drink.

"Do you know a man named Mark Stone?" I asked her.

She didn't respond. For a moment I wondered if she were still breathing. You can't go out on me at this moment, baby, I wanted to shout at her. I wanted to shake her into opening her eyes. I didn't do either. I went on talking in a quiet, conversational tone.

"He's head of security for Krider Industries," I said. "He

was here once, at the time that Mr. X came after Wilfred Krider and I got in his way. I think he talked to you then."

No response, no sign of life.

"Did the Old Man ever talk to you about Stone?"

Nothing.

"He talked to me. He had doubts about Stone. He thought Stone might have changed loyalties—shifted his support to someone else in Krider Industries. He even thought Mr. X might have been working for Stone, which would explain how Mr. X got by the guards that time."

She hadn't, didn't move a muscle.

"I keep thinking, luv, that Stone may be behind what's going on here. He's looking for something he thinks you have, or I have. Why he's waited five years to come after it I can't guess. Please, *please,* Duchess, try to remember if the Old Man gave you something to keep for him. Try to remember if he ever talked to you about Stone."

She remained motionless, hands hanging down below the arms of her chair.

"Don't die on me!" I said.

Her eyes popped open, and I almost laughed with relief. "It's not that easy to die, Daniel," she whispered. "I know. I've tried. Just let me rest for a little."

I couldn't tell if she'd heard anything I'd asked her, but I realized she didn't have what it would take to answer.

"I'll give you a few hours, dear, but I'll have to come back. Don't lock me out when I do." I touched her pale cheek with the back of my hand and headed for the door.

"Daniel!" She'd made the effort to call out to me. I turned back. She was sitting straight up in the chair, as though she'd found some hidden strength.

"Yes, Duchess?" I said.

"Your life may depend on your not trusting Mark Stone," she said. Then she sank back into her almost comotose position.

I remember I stepped out into the hall, closing the Duchess's door. The illumination out there is provided by shaded wall fixtures, providing a soft light. I stood there staring at the door I'd just closed. Was the old lady playing games with me? Was her apparent exhaustion an act? Had she made up her mind not to share some information she had? I was her friend, though, and she hadn't been able to resist warning me against what might be a danger. She'd certainly heard what I'd been saying even if she hadn't had the energy to answer, question by question. If I were in danger so was she. We both had Krider connections.

More important was the danger to Laura Stark, who was being used to force my hand—which had nothing in it!

There was no traffic in the hallway or on the stairs going down to the lobby. The lobby, panelled like most of the public rooms, decorated by paintings from local artists which were changed every month or so, was deserted. I glanced into the TV room where the color TV set was dishing out a late, late movie. George Caruthers, the night clerk, was seated at the rear of the desk area. He was new only this past year, a young man handling two jobs. He was bookkeeper for a local hardware store in the daytime, and doubled as an accountant and night clerk at the Red Cardinal from midnight till six in the morning, when he was relieved. He didn't go back to the days when Krider was a nightly visitor. I knew from local chit-chat that he was Camden born, raised, and educated. Suddenly I was looking at everyone connected with the Red Cardinal with suspicion, but young Mr. Caruthers seemed a very unlikely candidate for the role of villain. He looked up from his work, nodded to me, and returned to his figures and his little desk calculator.

There were still cheery voices coming from the lounge and I crossed the lobby and went in. It had only thinned out a little since I'd gone upstairs with the Duchess. Dick Carson and Chips were both missing, but the two golfers, the Townsend couple, and a dozen other regulars and guests were still keeping Dave Palmer, the bartender, busy. If there were any troopers still around the inn or its grounds they weren't visible here.

I crossed over to the bar and had Dave Palmer make me a short Jack Daniels on the rocks.

"Old lady know anything helpful?" Dave asked, as he put my drink down in front of me on a small paper napkin.

"Nothing," I said. "Where's Dick?"

"I thought he was with you," Dave said.

So Dick hadn't come back to where the people were. Chips had to sleep sometime. He came on with the earliest day crew at five in the morning. I wanted to talk to someone, but I didn't know who to talk to or what the hell to talk to them about. Not that I had anything to tell anyone that could be helpful to the opposition. I was faced with a simple disastrous fact. Demands were being made, with Laura's life at stake, that I had no way of meeting. I could wait till ten o'clock in the morning when that voice would contact me again on the phone. I'd have nothing to offer him. Was I to just sit around for nine hours—eight and a half hours now—and tell the voice, when it called, that I was awfully sorry but I still didn't know what he was talking about? Did I have any chance at all of persuading him that I was telling the truth?

I sat staring down into my drink, not really wanting it. I was ready for action, eager for it, but I didn't know where to find it. Kriders! Should I go up the Mountain and pull the crippled Maxwell out of his bed and demand to know what his late father had had that would fit into a coffee cup or the toe of a shoe? Was there any chance that Eleanore Krider would react to such a question? Should I toss Josh around a few times in the hope that he had something to spill? Not much promise in any of that.

Mark Stone? The Duchess had come out of her trance to warn me about him. But why had Mark Stone waited five years after the Old Man's death to send someone looking for something? Why, if Mr. X had been working for Stone ten years ago, had Stone had him killed here on Monday?

An elaborate notion began to percolate in my head. I had been close to Wilfred Krider. The Duchess had been very close to him. But there were others, weren't there? Dick Carson had been able to buy the Red Cardinal for a dollar, provided he took care of the Duchess for the rest of her life. Chips had known the Old Man for years longer than I had. Wilfred Krider had reason to trust them both before I'd ever come on the scene. If Krider wanted something kept safe for him in those early days wouldn't it have been logical for him to turn to Dick or Chips for help? If it were something that could turn out to be so vital to someone now, something for which lives could be taken and threatened, how logical was it to assume that Krider would have given it to the woman he loved to keep? His whole life had been dedicated to protecting her, keeping her safe. Was it sensible that he would make her the keeper of something that would endanger her survival? She didn't have whatever it was because he'd never given it to her, would never have placed her in a risk situation. He hadn't chosen me to guard his secret, whatever it was, because he'd already chosen someone else to be its custodian.

The Duchess, I told myself, was telling the truth. She had no more idea than I did what the voice on the telephone was asking us to produce.

I took a sip of my drink. It tasted a little better; I guess because I'd done away with one doubt. The Duchess was on the level, there was nothing wrong with her memory. There was nothing for her to remember.

When a cop's mind starts to fantasy solutions it's apt to

run out of control. When you think you're on the track of something you let her go Gallagher. So there was someone here, Dick or Chips or someone I hadn't thought of, who knew what it was that would fit in the toe of a shoe because he had it! That led to another cheerful thought. Suppose the Old Man's suspicions had been solid, and suppose Mr. X had been working for Mark Stone. Now, all this time later, Stone sends Mr. X here to find the object that will fit in a shoe. He doesn't know who has the object, but there are some likely possibilities. There is the Duchess, and so Mr. X plays TV repair man and comes up empty. There is me. There is someone else. After that TV repair man game, Mr. X goes to that someone else who actually has what he's looking for. That someone else shoots Mr. X in front of his left ear, hides the body—in this inn he knows so well—and waits for a chance to be rid of it.

Stone gets word from me, for God sake, that his man is dead and hasn't found what he came after. Who is a fast man with a gun in this neck of the woods? Me. If I shot Mr. X then I still have the object, and so my house is searched, my dog is killed, my woman is kidnapped. My move, since I am obviously it, with my friend the Duchess as an ally if I want to pass the object to someone else.

I finished my drink. There was one hole in this little opera I'd invented. If Mr. X had been sent here by Stone to find the object, he must have been told by Stone who might have it; the Duchess, me, and someone else. Stone knows who that someone else is, of course. Now he turns the heat on me and the Duchess. Has he sent the same message to that "someone else"—produce the object or the girl gets it? Is that someone else sweating it out now, just as I am? He's got more to sweat about than I have if my libretto is accurate. He has killed a man to keep that object out of Stone's hand^ How far will he go to protect Laura? If preserving a secret is worth one life, what about another?

I had at least two people to find in a very short time. I had to find the "someone else" who had killed Mr. X to save what could be hidden in the toe of a shoe. I had to find him to persuade him that no secret was worth keeping if it would cost Laura.

I had to find a second person who had searched my place and come back later to kidnap Laura. I had to find that one while Laura was still useful to Stone as a bargaining pawn. Because, and I tried to turn it off and couldn't, this person was someone who moved around freely in this area, not a stranger, probably someone well-known around the Red Cardinal. That meant the kidnapper was familiar enough to Laura so that he could lure her out of my house without waking me and that meant he could never let her go.

Three

Eight hours left.

I could get plastered, which would eventually induce sleep. I could set my alarm so that I'd be up in time to receive the kidnapper's call at ten o'clock. I could tell him I hadn't been able to turn anything up for him. After that I could never live with myself again when Laura's dead body turned up somewhere. There had to be something to *do*! You could fail, but you couldn't live with yourself if you hadn't tried.

Tried what, for Pete's sake?

Dave Palmer was getting ready to close up. He signaled to a young bar-boy who was carrying drinks to the tables. "Last call!" The voices behind me were gay, and there was a lot of laughter. There could be some bastard there, watching me, wondering what my gambit was going to be.

Then, I had an idea. Mark Stone could be, and unless I was all wet was, the villain of the piece. One thing was certain. He wasn't here, not in the open. His was a face I would never forget, although I'd only seen him once. But if he had someone here working for him he must be in touch, wanting to know how the Duchess and I were reacting to the kidnapper's phone call; how that "someone else" was reacting, assuming as I did that he, too, had had a call. Maybe if I could reach Stone, play it innocent, I could at least convince him that the Duchess and I didn't have what he wanted. Perhaps that would give Laura a little more time. If he knew that there were no safety deposit boxes to be emptied when the banks opened he'd have to play it another way, a way that would keep Laura off the front burner for longer than the time he'd given us.

I said goodnight to Dave and got out of there. My hackles were up, but good. I didn't look around to see if anyone was paying any particular attention to me, but I could almost feel somebody's eyes glued on me as I walked into the lobby. Clint Eastwood was slugging somebody out on the TV set in the sideroom, watched by no one. I had been a kind of *Dirty Harry* in my day, and right then I'd have given a good deal to apply a little muscle to someone. The problem was, who?

The pool was deserted. The moon, high overhead, had no one to look at tonight. I started across the lawn toward the highway and my cottage. Only two or three bedroom lights were burning on the upper floors of the inn. Except for the Red Cardinal the town of Camden had pretty well turned in for the night, darkened houses bathed in the silvery moonlight.

A cop's caution took charge of me and I walked up the driveway to the front door of my cottage. Mark Stone commanded an army. There could well be more than one person taking orders from him in this sleeping town.

I took my gun out of its holster and slid it into my jacket pocket, my right hand wrapped around it. Some bastard could be waiting for me in that dark cottage and I wasn't going to give him any edge at all, if he existed. I decided to go around to the kitchen door. It didn't make too much sense, because if he were watching me from a window, the bright moonlight would show him exactly what I was doing.

I stepped into the kitchen and stood there, in the darkness, gun out of my pocket. The stillness was almost oppressive. I don't know if I can make it clear how the house felt. The place where you live is private, personal, a safety zone. But once someone has broken in, taken it apart, gone through all your belongings, it doesn't have the same feel anymore. It was a danger place, not a safe place.

I reached up and pulled the chain to the fluorescent ceiling fixture that lit the kitchen. It was just as I had left it, pots and pans scattered around, drawers pulled out, kitchen silver dumped on the floor. I had closed the icebox door and it was humming, contentedly.

I moved into the living room, turned on lights—and on into the two bedrooms and the two baths. I looked in closets. There was no one waiting for me, but the place felt hostile.

I went back into the kitchen, made coffee in the percolator and plugged it in. Then I walked into the living room again and sat down at the telephone. I dialed Mark Stone's long-remembered number. I supposed it was to his office in the Krider Building on Madison Avenue in New York. There wasn't too much chance that he'd be there at 2:15 in the morning, but there might be some kind of answering service.

An impersonal female voice answered on the second ring. "Mr. Stone's office." Krider Industries operates all over the world in all the different time zones. This was, I supposed, an emergency number.

"My name is Dan Burton," I said. "Mr. Stone knows me. It's urgent that I reach him."

"I'll see if I can connect you with him," the operator said.

I waited what must have been four or five minutes. Then Stone came on.

"Do you have the faintest idea what time of night it is?" he asked, in his cold, emotionless voice.

"Exactly 2:19 A.M.," I said. I figured that was the right kind of answer for that kind of question.

"Well?" he said.

"I don't know how closely you've been staying in touch with the situation up here in Camden," I said.

"I haven't been staying in touch," he said. "You had a murder. The police don't know who the victim was or who the murderer is. It's a police job, none of my business."

"Maybe it is," I said, "because I think it's Krider business. You do still work for Krider Industries, don't you?"

"You know I do."

"So let me bring you up to date," I said. I outlined what had happened since I'd last talked to him. The Duchess's place searched again, her Teddy bear stolen, insides reamed out, discarded in the trash. My place searched, my dog killed, a girl, who offered to keep an eye on things while I slept, kidnapped. A phone call demanding something from us, not identified by the kidnapper. Time given us; until an hour after the banks open.

"Miss Walton and I just don't have the slightest idea what the creep is talking about," I said. "Since we were both close to Krider we have to think it relates to him in some way. From the nature of the search of my place we have to think it's a small object. Miss Walton swears the Old Man never gave her anything to keep for him. I know damn well he never gave me anything. We have no way to move to meet the kidnapper's demands."

"You mentioned banks opening," Stone said. He was at least interested.

"The kidnapper mentioned banks. He will call me an hour after the banks open this morning. We guess he thinks we may be keeping something in a safety deposit box. I don't have one. Miss Walton has one in the Manhattan Trust in New York, but there is nothing in it. Krider rented it for her years ago, but she's never used it."

"She says."

"She says!"

There was a long silence and then he spoke again in that flat, uninterested voice. "Let me tell you something, Burton," he said. "There are no Kriders involved in Krider Industries. Maxwell Krider has a large block of stock, derives his income from it, but neither he, nor his wife, nor his son have anything to do with the management, the policy, the direction of the corporation. I have to admit that the Old Man had his finger in the pie for a long time after his death. His estate has only just been probated about a month ago. There were complicated provisions that had to be carried out, all of which affected corporate policy. But that's over and done. Krider's board of directors now runs the corporation without any further input from the Old Man or any other Krider. A new president is about to be elected at the next board meeting—the end of the month. The Krider influence, the Krider policies, the Krider control are all as dead as the Old Man himself. I cannot conceive how anything that's going on up there in Camden can have anything to do with Krider Industries. If I could I'd be there for breakfast."

"I recommend the chicken hash this week," I said.

He made an impatient sound. "I don't know how I can help you or the state police," he said.

"What about Krider's private life? Some relationships outside the business?"

"Hell, man, Miss Walton was his private life," Stone said. "You know that. If anyone knows anything about his private world she does. You were as close to his comings and goings for ten years as anybody. Why ask me about it?"

"Because, dammit, you're a master of double talk, and trickery, and under-the-table games!"

"That's my job," he said, quietly.

"So what do I do when this turkey calls at ten o'clock? I don't know what he wants, so I don't know how to look for it. He's read Miss Walton and me wrong when he assumes we, or one of us, will instantly know what he's talking about. I'm sure you've dealt with extortionists in your time, Stone, protecting your billionaire board of directors. They must be some of the greatest targets for blackmail on earth. How do you deal with a man who won't tell you what he wants to be paid in—dollars, francs, yen, green stamps?"

I was playing my side of the game just as strong as I knew how. If Stone was the mastermind behind what was going on up here I had to convince him that the Duchess and I—Scout's honor—really didn't know what he wanted. I didn't care if he guessed I might suspect him. I was lost if he thought I knew what he expected from me.

What am I talking about, 'I was lost!' Laura was lost!

He didn't speak for so long that I shouted his name into the phone. "Stone! Are you still there?"

"I'm here," he said, in that dead voice. More silence, and then he spoke, like a man who doesn't put his foot forward until he's sure where he's stepping; separating each word as though it needed careful selection. "I don't care for guesswork, Burton. What is stored in the computers at Krider, and in my head, is mine—for my own use."

"A completely innocent girl may be dead before lunch," I said. My own voice was unsteady from anger, frustration, and a deep fear for Laura. There was one thing I couldn't say to this bastard on the other end of the line. I couldn't tell him that if anything happened to Laura I would, personally, go after him, with or without proof of his involvement. He'd been playing with the lives of human beings, guilty or innocent, for far too long. That was the name of the game. Then I had an unpleasant thought as I waited for him to go on. He was paid to decide whether people could live or die. But the Old Man, whom I had kept alive for ten years, had invented the game and made Stone what he was.

"I will share something with you because your problem intrigues me," Stone said. "What I'm going to tell you is not a secret anymore because it's no longer true. But in the days when the Old Man was in power Krider Industries was an outsized version of the Oval Office in the Nixon White House. Every place where anything of any interest to Wilfred Krider could happen was bugged; offices, closets, washrooms, elevators—every place you could imagine in the Krider Building. And round the world—in the Shah's palace in Iran, or 10 Downing Street for all I know. The men who worked for me were wired for sound. The house on Camden Mountain was wired for sound. How do you suppose he knew you were having an affair with Eleanore Krider? Your bedroom was bugged. Miss Walton's room at the Red Cardinal was bugged—in case she decided to crawl into the hay with a visiting fireman—or you, or Carson, or whoever."

"You knew about Eleanore Krider?" I asked, shocked.

"I spent my life listening to thousands of miles of tapes with Krider. That is how his business and private strategies were developed. I had a small army of technicians who kept hundreds of listening devices working, stenographers who transcribed the tapes for files that would fill a building—until they became obsolete."

"So what has all this got to do with the price of eggs?" I asked. My bedroom at *Hilltop* bugged! Someone listening to all the nonsense Eleanore and I had talked to each other! Some silly stenographer giggling over us as she transcribed the tape! The Old Man, my friend, my benefactor, had been a low grade bastard! A peeping, listening Tom!

"What it has to do with the price of eggs," the flat, cold voice said, "is that a small cassette tape would fit in a coffee cup, or the toe of a shoe—or the insides of a teddy bear. It isn't impossible at all, Burton, that the Old Man gave an incriminating tape to someone to keep for him. That may be what your kidnapper is after."

"And waited five years after the Old Man died to come looking for it?"

"Bear in mind," Stone said, "that it is only a month ago that his records, files, tapes, were finally cleaned up and cleared out. The man who's interested knows, at last, that what he wants wasn't in the corporation records. Where else to look but the house where Krider lived on Camden Mountain, the inn where his mistress still lives, the town where his ex-bodyguard lives? It could be that way. People the Old Man trusted would follow his instructions long after he died."

The dial tone buzzed in my ear. Was Stone telling me something he knew, or had he just dreamed it up? Had he cleverly set me up to find his tape for him? It was better than having no ideas at all.

I sat there, staring at the phone, angry. I felt betrayed by Krider. He had trusted me, I thought. Well, he'd had reason to trust me - my phone bugged, my bed bugged! Over ten years he must have had quite a collection on me. Did he keep them, like a memory-book, or were they wiped out and set up again once he'd heard them? I wondered if he'd had a tape of my passage with the housemaid at *Hilltop,* or one of me singing in the shower. It was like learning I'd been naked in front of him for ten years.

So cool it, I told myself. He left you a half a million bucks. You could walk out on him right now and there was no way he could take it back. Or could he—in the sense that he could see to it that I didn't enjoy it? I was still working for him, looking out for the Duchess. There could be others still working for him, seeing to it that I carried out his wishes, that the Duchess carried out his wishes. A watching B who watches C who is watching A! He was still maneuvering us after he was dead. If Stone were right, by guess or by certain knowledge, there was a tape somewhere that someone needed to protect himself—or to use against someone. It was a tape important enough to justify risking murder, a kidnapping, and almost certainly a second murder. Laura couldn't be let go because she would be able to name her kidnapper.

Laura was what mattered right now. I could settle with the Old Man for playing dirty pool with me in the next world. Laura was in the trouble she was in because of my association with him. If Mark Stone, the general of Wilfred Krider's old army, was prepared to help find Laura, save her, he hadn't given me any indication of it. If Stone himself were the villain I could only hope I'd persuaded him that the Duchess and I didn't know where to find what he wanted.

There was, however, someone who did know where to look; the someone who had shot Mr. X in front of his left ear and dumped him in the Red Cardinal's pool. Mr. X must have been looking in the right place when he got his. That right place was not in my house. It was across the street, somewhere in that gracious, old, rambling country inn or in its scattering of outbuildings. The person who had killed Mr. X was there, and the person who had kidnapped Laura. And I was sitting here on my behind in a crossfire between them, doing nothing, with just a little more than seven hours left before it would be too late.

I got up from the phone, loosened my gun in its holster, and walked out of my house into the moonlight.

Like my house, violated and searched by a stranger, the Red Cardinal had lost its familiar, comfortable feel. There were only a few lights, one outside the front entrance, one or two in the lobby area, one bedroom on the second floor. The dark windows were no longer welcoming. Somewhere behind them was violence, and violent men.

I walked up onto the porch of the inn and let myself into the lobby. I crossed over to the desk. George Caruthers, the accountant-night clerk, was busy with his desk calculator. He looked pleased to take a break with someone to talk to.

"Anything new, Mr. Burton?" he asked.

"What's new is the miracle of sleep," I said. I was being consumed by an anger that seemed to grow with the passing of time. "Everybody in this damned place goes quietly off to bed while a girl is being held for ransom, maybe somewhere on the grounds. Don't faint if they send you her left ear for breakfast."

"Like that young guy that was kidnapped in Italy," he

said, his eyes bright.

"Like that," I said.

"The troopers have been all over the inn," he said. "Every room, the catacombs, everywhere. She sure isn't here, Mr. Burton."

I should have known Captain Folwell would be thorough. Somehow it didn't make me feel any better.

"Where is Dick Carson?" I asked.

"I haven't seen him for about an hour," George said. "I think he's in his cottage."

"Sleeping—while Rome burns," I said.

"Gee, Mr. Burton, he hasn't had any sleep since night before last! He's just plain pooped out, I think."

So everybody is pooped out, so we'll all worry about Laura tomorrow! Action was what I wanted and I was going to get it.

I walked past the darkened lounge and into the dining room. A single light burned over the door that led to the serving pantry. The room was in perfect shape for breakfast, places set at the tables, napkins folded in little standing cones. You have a murder and a kidnapping but you're still in the country inn business.

I went into the pantry. I knew there was a door at the back of it that led out into the parking lot. Dishes and glasses and silverware were neatly stacked on a long, stainless steel table, ready for the morning rush. I went to the door at the rear and out into the crowded parking lot. At the far end of it was Dick's place, a small cottage with lilac bushes in front.

There was a light in the window. I cupped my hands around my eyes and looked inside. Dick was there, sitting at a stretcher table that was stacked with bills, receipts, mail, trade magazines. His arms were folded on the table, his head resting on them. He had fallen asleep at whatever he was doing. I knocked on the screen frame and he sat up, abruptly, his eyes bleary and bloodshot.

"Come in!" he called out. When he saw it was me he waved

at the stuff on the table. "I lose track of how much Ruth does for this operation till she's gone. I'm snowed under, what with my work, and hers, and now all this hullabaloo."

Ruth was his life support system, I guess. "How is her mother?"

He made a seesaw gesture with his hands. "Any news?" he asked.

"Did you know your inn was bugged?" I asked him, and sat down in a chair across the table from him.

"What the hell are you talking about?"

I reminded him of Mark Stone. He'd met the security man when we'd had our first encounter with Mr. X.

"I called him, because if this is a Krider thing, and I think it is, he might have answers."

"And did he?" Dick seemed suddenly very wide awake.

"I learned that Wilfred Krider's life was ordered by electronically listening to everyone and every place that might be of any interest to him. He told me the Duchess's suite was bugged. Who knows, there may have been listening ears in your private john."

"I knew about the Duchess's rooms—and so did she," he said. He looked tired again. I was telling him old stuff.

"It was apparently some kind of a fetish with him," I said. "It seems my room in his own house was bugged—my bedroom! It pleased him to listen in on my sex life. Stone thinks that's why he had the Duchess wired for sound."

"That's nonsense," Dick said. He reached for a cigarette in a pack on the table. His hands weren't too steady when he lit it. "Martha was over seventy years old when he installed that taping gadget in her room."

"I imagine she was pretty much alive at seventy," I said.

"They were in love," Dick said, sounding impatient. "I never saw two people so in love. For God sake, are you blind, Dan? You saw it."

"I was in love with him, too," I said, sourly. "He bugged me."

"His safety was in your hands," Dick said. "He had to be sure of you. He lived in the world of the double-triple-cross! Martha he loved with all his heart."

"So why?"

"He told me. He told her," Dick said. "He was always afraid someone would try to get at him through her."

"Get at him?"

"A kidnapping, violence of some sort. If anything happened to her there would be a tape of it. It was a way of defending her. According to him, he and everyone he cared about was a perpetual target."

"So why didn't he have someone here to protect her?"

"Aren't you here?"

"Before he died," I said. "She was here for fifteen years before he died. While he was alive I was with him, on Camden mountain. Why wasn't there someone here to guard her if he felt that way?"

"Wilfred Krider ran his own world," Dick said. His smile was wry. "And mine, and yours. Until the old lady conks out he controls us both."

"Your inn and my bankroll," I said. "Well, let me tell you something, chum. You seem to be running a summer home for killers and kidnappers. The only loyalty I have at this moment is to Laura Stark. She's taking the rap for me, for the Duchess, for God knows who else. I got her into it."

"How?"

"By hanging around her, mooning over her, making her feel sorry for me—putting her in the mood to do me a favor—to let me have a couple of hours' sleep without my finger inside the trigger guard of this gun." I slapped at my shoulder holster.

"I'm sorry. I know how you must feel, but—."

"There are no buts about it. They didn't carry her away from my place and down the street on a Miss America float. She's here somewhere, Dick. Or what's left of her is here. They can't let her go, you know. She didn't walk out of my house, unprotesting, with a stranger."

He sat there, silent, letting that soak in.

"Stone suggests that what Mr. X was looking for in the Duchess's rooms, what someone was looking for in my place, was one of Wilfred Krider's tapes. It would fit in the small places they searched."

"A tape of what?"

"How the hell do I know? A tape that can put someone behind the eight ball. Either someone is looking for it to save his own neck, or to use it to put someone else out of business. It's worth enough to kill for it."

Dick was looking past me, out his screened window toward his blessed inn. "The Duchess ever play you any of her tapes?" he asked.

It was my turn to look at him with my jaw hanging loose.

"Her tapes? What tapes?" I said.

"Like you said, the Old Man was tape-oriented," Dick said. "I don't remember exactly how long ago it was, but he gave the Duchess a cassette player. There are a couple of boxes of tapes hidden under all that junk in her front room."

"Tapes of what? His business transactions? My sex life?"

"Songs she used to sing, back in her show business days," Dick said. "I imagine she recorded on records originally for Victor or someone like that. He had them taken off on tape. They have processes for improving the quality of the sound, you know. I've never heard any of them, but I've seen the little boxes she keeps the tapes in with the titles of the songs written on them—"A Pretty Girl Is Like A Melody," "Just My Bill," "Summertime," songs like that from back then. They used to play them when he came to spend an evening with her. Their songs, I suppose you'd say. The songs that went with their love affair. As far as I know she never played them for anyone else."

I was a cop again, not an angry man. That old Chesterton story popped back into my mind. "Where would you hide a leaf? In a forest." Krider could have given the Duchess a tape to keep, shuffled in with her other tapes. Or he could have just put it there himself without telling her. Could be Mr. X had been right on target. Had he found it, been shot, and relieved of it? Not likely, I thought. He must have missed it, if it were there, or else why had someone been searching my place for it two days later?

"Maybe we better go listen to music," I said to Dick.

Part Three

One

Dick and I stopped at the desk where he picked up a key ring with a big wooden tag attached to it, a dozen or more keys.

"She isn't going to answer a knock at this time of night," Dick said. "I have an understanding with her. In an emergency I use the passkey."

"What kind of an emergency?"

"Fire." He gave me a quick, sidelong glance. "Death."

"Death?"

"At ninety-four, Dan, you just might not wake up some morning. It is agreed that only I will use the passkey." His smile was almost tender. "In case of death she doesn't want anyone else to find her looking awkward or ugly. I had to cross my heart on that one."

The old girl still had her vanity. Vanity of a nice kind, I thought. She didn't want anyone to suffer the shock of seeing her off guard, unprepared.

We climbed the red-carpeted stair to the second floor and knocked on the Duchess's door. As Dick had predicted, she didn't answer. We tried several more times, giving her plenty of time to gather herself together, climb out of bed, put on a robe and come to the door. Finally Dick used the passkey and went in.

The jumble room was dark, but some kind of soft night light was burning inside the open door of the bedroom. We hadn't taken a step into the room before she called out.

"Richard? Is that you?"

"Yes, Martha. Dan's with me."

"Oh, lord!" It was a long, weary, sighing sound. "Turn on the lights. The switch is right there by the door."

"I know, dear. It's my inn," Dick said.

"Give me a minute or two," she called out.

Dick switched on the lights, shaded lamps that all worked from the one control. The familiar confusion welcomed us. It was her home, her place, her style, her character.

We waited, listening to slow movements in the bedroom. More lights went on there and I could picture her sitting in front of her theatrically lighted dressing table mirror. She wasn't to be seen with curlers in her hair or cold cream on her face. I doubted if she'd bothered with any of that when she went to bed, she'd been so done in.

At last she appeared in the doorway. Her henna-colored hair was brushed out, hanging loosely to her shoulders. The little spots of rouge were at her cheeks, the pale blue tint on her eyelids, lipstick carefully applied. She was wearing a wine-colored housecoat that fell down to the tips of her silver slippers. She was not carelessly prepared to meet two gents at three o'clock in the morning.

"You asked me not to ignore a knock, Daniel," she said. "But I—I needed just a little more time. I hoped you'd go away and come back somewhat later. But now that you're here—" She gestured vaguely toward chairs that really weren't meant to sit in. They were catch-alls for junk. She sat down on her "throne" leaned her head back, and closed her eyes.

"I'm sorry to have routed you out," I said. "But we think we know what this may be all about—what the kidnapper wants. A cassette tape."

The blue eyes lifted and she looked at me steadily, but she didn't speak.

I tried to make what Stone had suggested make sense to her. Tapes had been so much a part of Wilfred Krider's world. There could be one in existence that was a threat to someone.

A tape could have been hidden in the kind of places they had searched in my house. Now Dick had told me that she had a cassette player and a collection of tapes. That would explain what Mr. X had been looking for, not found,since my place had been searched much later.

"Is it possible, dear, that the Old Man gave you a tape to keep for him?" I asked her.

"He brought me tapes from time to time," she said, after a moment. "But they were all tapes of the same performer — me. It amused him to look for old recordings in record shops. Back in the twenties before records were such a huge business, I recorded quite a few songs — twenty or twenty-five, I think — that I sang in shows and in my nightclub act. Will loved them. He had a place where they'd transfer them to tape and they sounded quite a lot better than the records. When he found one we didn't have he'd bring me the tape, and we'd play it." The blue eyelids lowered again. She was remembering a pleasure that had meant a great deal to her. "I wasn't a Nora Bayes, or a Ruth Etting, or a Helen Morgan," she said. "But I was — pretty damn good!" She opened her eyes and smiled at me.

"I'll bet you were," I said.

"Can we look at your collection of tapes to see if there is one there that isn't a performance of yours, Martha?" Dick asked.

"You want me to arrange a concert for you?" she asked.

"It's possible, isn't it, Martha, that in those boxes of tapes of yours there may be one the Old Man stuck in there without your knowing?" Dick asked her.

"Unless he came back and did it yesterday, or the day before — " she said, and let it hang there.

"Are you telling us you check them over that often?" I asked.

"Age, age, age," she said. "You won't know anything about growing old, Daniel, until you get there yourself. Some people survive it by going on with whatever their work is until the day they die. Others, for one reason or another, quit doing their thing early—or reasonably early. Maybe they take up a hobby. They live in their past and in their hobby. That's me. I was good enough at what I did to have my name up in lights on the front of a Broadway theater. I quit when I was forty-four. Maybe that was right, because I was selling feminine charm, physical beauty. In any case, I took up a hobby—Will Krider. Making love to him, making him happy and fulfilled was my hobby. I guess you could say I was a success at it. I had my name up in lights on the front of his theater for forty-five years. For the last five years I've lived in that second half of my life." She gestured around the jumbled room. "Newspaper clippings about Will, magazine stories about Will, gifts he gave me, these tapes you're so interested in which he had made for me, jewelry he slipped on my fingers, my wrists, and fastened around my neck. 'Have you lost any jewelry, Miss Walton?' I know I haven't, because I handle those things every day. 'Is there a tape you didn't know you had, Miss Walton?' Of course there isn't, because I look at them each day of my life. There are exactly thirty-four of them, twenty-six songs. I made second recordings of eight songs which accounts for the difference. Will found them all long before he died."

"You play them every day?" I asked.

"I haven't played any of them since Will died," she said. "But I handle the little boxes every day, just as I handle the other things he gave me—including poor Teddy."

"Could we look at the tapes, darlin'?" I persisted, as gently as I could.

"Every tape is labeled," she said. "There's no unexplained one there."

"Were there any songs the Old Man didn't like?" I asked her. "Ones you didn't play over for him?"

She smiled at me. "You want me to run myself down?" she asked. "He loved them all. Well—he had his choices amongst the ones for which we had two tapes. "He's Just My Bill," for example. One of them was sung with a full orchestra, one with just a piano. He liked the piano one, so we never played the one with the orchestra. A couple of old George M. Cohan numbers; he liked them with the full brass of an orchestra—"Over There." We never played the one with just my accompanist behind me. "Hello, Frisco, Hello"—the old telephone song, remember? He had a choice on that one. Two or three others."

"Could we hear those tapes you didn't play over and over—the ones where the Old Man had his choice, a favorite?"

"What are you getting at, Daniel?"

"It's possible," I said, "that he palmed off something on you that he wanted to hide. A tape that someone will commit murder to get—or keep. Maybe the tape that's marked "Hello, Frisco, Hello"—the one he didn't like and that you didn't play—was replaced long ago by a tape that isn't you, one he wanted to hide."

"I'd know," she said, positively.

"How?"

"I'd just know, Daniel. Like I knew about the jewelry. If anything that belonged to me was gone I'd—I'd feel it in my bones?"

"Even if the Old Man took it—long ago?"

She shook her head slowly, from side to side. "Will would never have done such a thing without telling me. We had no secrets."

"You told me you knew nothing about his business. That was all kept from you."

"His business was his business. We had no secrets that concerned our lives together. He would never have planted something on me, specially something as dangerous as you say this is, without telling me. It's just not possible."

End of the line. Dead end street.

"Will you let us listen to those tapes you didn't play over and over?"

"We'd have to listen to them all, wouldn't we, Dan?" Dick put in. "After five years of no play it's possible—I mean—"

"That I'm a crazy old bag who thinks she's psychic?" the Duchess said.

"Duchess, if I didn't try everything I could think of, no matter how impossible, and it cost Laura Stark her life, I'd just have to—to ride off into that sunset," I said.

"You think it's as bad as that?" she asked.

"I think I've got to find her—or what they want—before they call later this morning or Laura will have had it. It may be too late anyhow' but there's a chance we could deal if we had something to deal with."

I don't know if it took her a full minute to make up her mind, or whether it was simply because she needed that much time to gather the strength to stand up out of her chair.

She crossed the room to a stack of newspapers that came up to her waist. She began moving the papers to an adjoining chair. She seemed to take great care with them as though she knew exactly what order they were in. Buried in the pile were two small cardboard boxes. In the boxes were the thirty-four tapes, each in little colored paper containers. There was a label on each one, just the title of the song.

"Nobody had ever heard these but Will," she said. "I think he wouldn't mind. She's a nice girl—and very gifted." She handed me the boxes. "And you'd better take the cassette player, too, or you won't be able to hear them."

The player turned out to be in the drawer of a desk.

"You'll let us take them somewhere to listen to them?" I asked.

"My God, you think I want to sit here for an hour or two, listening to myself?" she said. "Not without Will."

She might not have been a Nora Bayes, or a Ruth Etting, or a Helen Morgan, but she sure enough was Martha Walton, with her own style, her own enormous energy, her own special flare for phrasing.

Dick and I had taken the tapes and the player to his place. We soon discovered that the eight tapes that Wilfred Krider hadn't liked as much as their duplicates were all marked with a little check. I thought they were great, and when I listened to the duplicates he'd liked, I wasn't sure I agreed with his taste. One thing was certain. The Old Man had taken a real star out of circulation when she was probably just at her prime. He must have really been something to turn her off her career. She'd had it made.

It was nearly five o'clock in the morning when we'd played them all and come up with a zero. There was nothing there that wasn't advertised on the little colored packages. Most of the recordings didn't take up the full length of the tape, but nothing had been recorded on those unused portions. We had heard a really great singer perform for two hours and come up empty.

We sat looking at each other across Dick's table desk.

"I'm glad you had the idea," Dick said, "but where are we?"

"Out at sea in a rowboat without any oars," I said. I brought my fist down on the table. "Dammit, Dick, someplace where we could reach out and touch him is a kidnapper. Laura could never have been conned out of my house by a stranger."

"You've said that before."

"And I'm still convinced. She knew I was wearing a gun. I think it shocked her. It certainly satisfied her I was looking for real trouble. She was there to wake me if there was something wrong. Would she have gone outside to talk to a stranger?"

"I have to think not," Dick said.

"So it had to be someone from this bloody inn, someone who saw her cross the street to my house, someone who wondered why she stayed so long and came over to check, probably after dark. He sees me asleep, sees her sitting in the living room, probably reading, taps on the window and signals her to come out. Because she knows him she goes. Not just someone who hung around her piano. Someone she knows and trusts. Someone she thinks is *my* friend!"

He grinned at me. "You have friends?"

I wasn't in the mood. "I used to think so. Friends like you," I said.

His face muscles tightened. "Now, easy, Dan!"

"Well, she would have come out to you, friend. She would have gone out to Chips, to Dave Palmer, the night bartender, to one of your aunts."

"You surely don't think Miss Anne or Miss Amy is a kidnapper?"

"If Mark Stone is behind all this he could buy anyone," I said. "Price wouldn't matter to him. Miss Anne or Miss Amy could have gotten Laura out of my house for someone else to grab."

"You're dreaming, Dan!"

"What else can I do? It could be that way. Listen to me, Dick. Twenty-five years ago, before my time, before your time, Wilfred Krider set up his woman in this inn. If he was so damned afraid someone might try to get at him through her—your words, pal—he must have set up someone to guard her. Then, five years later, he sold you and Ruth the inn. You were to look out for the lady, see to her comfort, her meals, her service, her pleasures when he wasn't there. Were you told to guard her against some kind of violence?"

"No."

"Well, just as sure as hell somebody was. I came into the picture fiteen years ago. He was my responsibility, not the lady. He never once asked me to keep an eye on her until he was ready to die. I was to look out for her, but not in this sense of danger, after he was gone. There was someone else for that. If I had been meant to protect her from danger he'd have seen to it that I moved into the room across the hall. He would have briefed me on what the danger might be. He didn't do that. He didn't suggest that there was any danger, except that you might neglect her after he was gone. There was someone else, Dick. Someone else with whom he made a deal."

"We cleaned out the entire staff here when we took over," Dick said. "We didn't want people around telling us they knew how to run the inn better than we did. Whoever looked out for her before that was gone. If he made a deal with someone after that—?" He looked vague.

"If you don't know what's going on in your own place there's only one other person who might. Chips. Mr. Everything."

"I'd trust him with my life," Dick said. "And Ruth's."

"Maybe the Old Man trusted him with the lady's life," I said.

There is an old barn at the far end of the property, made over into a garage for inn machinery, lawn mowers, a small tractor, a snow plow for winter. On the second floor are a couple of apartments. That's a fancy word for them. They're just two rooms with an adjoining john. Chips occupies one of them. The other has had a series of tenants in my time. The present one was Dominic, the short-order chef, a pleasant Italian guy.

It was grey dawn when I climbed the stairs in that barn-garage to Chips' room. I pounded on the door, I went in. He wasn't there. His bed hadn't been slept in.

I tried Dominic, who was very sound asleep and a little resentful when I shook him awake.

"Chips hasn't slept here for three or four nights," he said. "He's in the inn somewhere, I think. He said on account of the trouble there."

"Three or four nights? There wasn't any trouble till last night."

Dominic shrugged. "I don't know. That's what he said.

Monday, I think."

"You know where he is in the inn?"

"He didn't say."

My watch told me it was just five o'clock as I crossed the parking lot through the growing daylight and went back into the inn. The television set was still going, soundlessly. I got a glimpse of Laurence Olivier and Martita Hunt in some long-ago English movie. Without sound the actors looked like ghosts.

George Caruthers, still at the desk, didn't know where Chips might be staying in the inn—didn't know that he was staying in the inn.

"He comes on a little after five, though," George told me. "You might find him in the kitchen. He usually gets his own breakfast there."

I went down the narrow stairway from the lobby to the catacombs. I was instantly assailed by the pleasant aroma of freshly baked bread. I remembered that Mrs. Kramer, the local woman who did the baking, began her daily chores in the very early hours of the morning. The catacombs were warmed by the heat from the baking ovens. I caught sight of Mrs. Kramer in her white apron. She was lifting something out of the oven on a giant spatula that looked almost as large as a canoe paddle.

"Chips?" I asked her.

She waved, vaguely, toward the other side of the kitchen. She was well on the way with her day's production of baked goods for the dining room and the Misses Quigley in the gift shop.

"I recommend the rye bread, if you like it," Mrs. Kramer said. "I'll give you a loaf for your house, if you say so."

"I'll stop back after I talk to Chips," I said.

The kitchen area is divided by the gas and electric ranges, the long stainless steel serving table, a couple of standing freezers, so that it looks like several rooms when, in reality, it is one large space. An exhaust fan turned lazily in the far wall.

I didn't see Chips, but on the serving table next to the gas range was an untouched plate of bacon and eggs, a couple of slices of buttered toast, a cup of coffee. I waited for Chips to appear out of one of the walk-in storage rooms where I assumed he had gone to get something to augment his ready breakfast. He didn't show.

I went back to the baking ovens where Mrs. Kramer was shoveling several pans of hard roll dough into the oven on her paddle.

"You see where Chips went?" I asked her.

She waved again in the direction of the untouched breakfast, withdrew her paddle from the ovens, and pushed the oven door shut. Then she turned and looked to where she thought Chips was.

"Search me," she said. "Probably somebody called him from upstairs. There's always some kind of emergency for Chips. He fixes everything, you know."

There are several wall phones in the kitchen. They connect with the dining room and the front desk. I tried one of them and found myself talking to George Caruthers.

"Chips isn't down here," I said. "Did somebody call him? He's left his breakfast untouched."

"Not through the board," Caruthers said.

Under normal conditions not finding Chips would have been no cause for alarm. His responsibilities were everywhere. That Friday morning, conditions in the Red Cardinal could not be called normal.

"Funny he'd leave his breakfast just sitting on the serving table," I said to Mrs. Kramer.

"I'll put it in the warming oven for him," the lady said.

"You're sure you didn't see him go?"

"My busy time," she said. She gestured toward her table, loaded down with breads and cakes.

"You didn't see anyone come in to speak to him?"

Mrs. Kramer looked annoyed with me. "Why should I, Mr. Burton? I got my work to do here. Up to my neck in it.

Who comes and goes I don't notice."

That was reasonable, I guessed. I walked down one of the semi-dark corridors that led to the store room and tool shop. I called to Chips. This was an area where he operated. I thought he might have remembered something he was going to need later, a tool, equipment of some sort, left his breakfast to get it. My voice seemed to echo off the old, thick walls. There was no response from Chips. I opened a couple of doors into unlighted, dark rooms, calling his name without any luck.

He must have gone into the "upper world" somewhere, I went back into the kitchens. Just as I got there Fritz Schlee, the giant chef, filled the doorway. Out of his white clothes and chef's hat he was still an impressive figure of a man, six-feet-three-or-four inches tall, muscular not fat it seemed, with a thin red beard and moustache that framed a perpetual and sardonic smile.

"You still looking for bodies?" he asked me.

"I was looking for Chips. He left his breakfast without eating it. I thought he might be in one of the workrooms back there."

"The police have taken up residence down here," Fritz said. "First they were looking for where the dead man's body was hidden. Then they look for a kidnapped girl. It is like working in a revolving door! Chips is somewhere. He is always somewhere, doing something nobody else can do—or will do!"

He turned to a closet where he kept his white working clothes and began to pull them on over the slacks and sport shirt he was wearing. I watched him, remembering his long ago outburst against Wilfred Krider. *"The man you work for is a butcher! And here I am preparing delicacies for his mistress!"*

I lit a cigarette and leaned against the thick stone wall, wondering. If Mark Stone had wanted someone to work for him here, work for him against Wilfred Krider's interests, this giant from Mittel-Europa with a hatred for the Kriders would have been prime beef on the hoof.

"You have theories about all this, Fritz?" I asked him.

"I think it is ironic," he said, his smile gone, "that five years after he is dead, Wilfred Krider still has men at each others' throats. In life he arranged for people to be butchered, and in death it still goes on."

"So you agree with me that all this is linked to the Kriders in some way?"

He shrugged his huge shoulders. "What else? A quiet country town, a few shops, services for the people whose homes are here, this inn—a place of quality. The only place of evil was up the mountain, while Wilfred Krider was still alive. Five years pass and there is violence again. Where does it focus? On Wilfred Krider's mistress, on you, his ex-bodyguard, on this inn, which he technically still owns until the old lady passes on and the property becomes, legally, Dick Carson's."

He seemed to know more of the facts than most people did.

"I do not wish anyone ill who is still alive," he said, "but if you and the old lady were harmed I would say you had inherited the wind! *'As ye sow, so shall ye reap.'* But that young girl, damn it, Mr. Burton, *that* I resent. She is like an innocent schoolchild, standing on a street corner, smashed down by a heartless hit-and-run driver. Like my parents! Like my family! They never knew the Kriders. They never did a Krider any harm. But they, along with hundreds of other innocents, got in the way of the Krider steamroller, left to rot by the roadside."

His anger was real, no act, I thought.

"You've been here, almost since the day Dick Carson took over," I said.

"Twenty years, three months," he said.

"There must not be an inch of this place you don't know well."

"I would think not."

He was fitting on his tall chef's hat. It turned him from an angry, perhaps dangerous man into an almost comic figure out of a TV commercial. But there was nothing comic about the white hot intensity I saw in his narrowed eyes.

"Someone Laura knew persuaded her to step outside my house without waking me," I said. "It had to be someone she knew and trusted."

He took a short step toward me and I braced myself. This was no one I wanted to slug it out with however hungry I was for action.

"Are you saying *me,* Mr. Burton, to get even with a dead man?"

"I'm asking who she knew and trusted on the staff," I said. "There was Dick Carson, and Chips, and you, I think. I've seen you standing in the corner of the bar at night while she played."

"No one plays Viennese waltzes anymore," he said. "She knows so many of them."

"Who else on the staff, Fritz? I know she was friendly with Ruth's aunts. But did she come down here to make food for herself? Had she made friends with Mrs. Kramer, or Dominic, or any of your other people?"

"People do not wander in and out of my kitchen, even my best friends—only troopers and detectives looking for bodies!" He exploded. "I promise you, Mr. Burton, when we find out who snatched that girl I will, personally, break him into five million pieces!"

"You say there's not an inch of this place you don't know. I think Laura is close by. Where have we failed to look, Fritz?"

"I wish I knew. If I could tell you I would look there myself. I do not want her hurt, Mr. Burton. If she is, I—I will have a new life's work! I will kill a man as slowly and painfully as it is possible to kill."

True or false, I wondered. It was a performance so big that Fritz seemed more like an actor in a melodrama than a man with real feelings.

"You told the police you'd never seen the man who was found in the pool. You were around here ten years ago when he tried to get Wilfred Krider."

"It is a pity you stopped him," Fritz said. "I know you

were doing your job. I didn't see him then. I didn't see him this time until he was dead." He shrugged. "I saw the likeness the police artist drew of him ten years ago, but I don't think I would have recognized him from that."

"People from Krider Industries' security investigated that attempt on the Old Man ten years ago. Did you get to know a man named Stone, Mark Stone, at that time?"

He gave me a level look. The actor playing a role again? "Stone? Not an uncommon name," he said. "But, no. I would remember the name of anyone connected with the Kriders."

"You've never treated me, Fritz, as though I was a villain," I said.

"You were a man with a gun, Mr. Burton," he said. "The gun was meant to protect Wilfred Krider, which was a pity. You didn't use that gun to butcher innocent people. You were decent with the people here in the inn. You never asked for special privileges, extra service, because the Krider money was behind you. You were not connected with Krider when my family was wiped out. You had no part in that."

"You were here for fifteen years while he was still alive," I said, "and you never made a move at him?"

He gave me that Machiavellian smile of his. "At least you had no way of sharing my dreams in those days, Mr. Burton. They didn't come true, but I dreamed them, nonetheless. You wouldn't have slept well if you'd been in on those dreams."

"We have so little time, Fritz. Where could they keep Laura—alive? The troopers have been over this plant from top to bottom. Yet I have the feeling she has to be close by—unless they simply killed her and dumped her somewhere."

He shook his head. "I wish I knew how to answer that, Mr. Burton."

"You don't know where Chips has gone? If anyone can come up with anything we haven't thought of it's Chips."

Fritz moved away from me toward his ranges and ovens. "I'll tell him you're looking for him when he comes back," he said.

When violence moves into your world it's like an infection. Nothing that has seemed normal in your everyday life seems normal anymore. If you have a cop's mind, and I do, no one is to be trusted. If there were one person in this world of the Red Cardinal I believed in it was Chips.

"I'd trust him with my life and Ruth's," Dick Carson had said.

I wouldn't trust any man with my life. As a cop, and a very young man, I mistrusted any man I saw walking toward me on the street. It was that kind of world. Then I went to work for Wilfred Krider, and the Old Man spent ten years educating me to believe that we live in a time when the sell-out, the double cross, is the normal. He lived that way himself and made no bones about it. He trusted me to protect his life—but he bugged my bedroom just to make sure. That was his philosophy, I guess. Your judgment tells you that some people can be trusted, but never all the way. You can buy loyalty if you'll pay enough, you can insure loyalty if you have something you can use to twist an arm. But you don't count on friendship or love.

Yet the Old Man had trusted Martha Walton, the Duchess. It was that trust that made her so precious to him, I thought. She was a unique experience in his world.

In the small world in which I'd lived the last fifteen years—the world of Camden, and the Red Cardinal Inn—there was one person I came close to trusting. I would have been genuinely shocked to learn that Chips was not on the level, that he could be bought. In this climate, turned dark by a murder and a kidnapping, Chips was the one person about whom I had no doubts. How dare he leave his breakfast to go to the john without telling someone where he was going? That's how absurd my thinking was just about then.

I climbed the stairs back to the lobby. I noticed that lights were turned on in the gift shop across the lobby. Cleaning people, I assumed, and went over there to talk to them. Anyone might have seen Chips.

In my state I was counting on Chips for answers he'd never suggested he had.

Very much to my surprise, the Quigley sisters were in the gift shop. Five-thirty in the morning was surely not their standard opening time. It certainly wasn't mine. I had never watched "the dawn come up like thunder" in all the time I'd lived in these parts. To be more accurate, I may have come home from an all-night party at daylight, but I had never gotten up this early to start a day.

The Quigley sisters were busily straightening their wares.

"Oh, Mr. Burton!" one of them cried when she saw me.

"The bearer of good tidings, I hope." the other said.

I never can be sure which is Anne and which is Amy till I'm clued in.

"We couldn't sleep," the first one said.

"Anne couldn't sleep," Miss Amy said.

So I had the right handles on them. "I'm looking for Chips," I said. "Have either of you ladies seen him? I thought he might be helping you to open up for business."

"Oh, we're not open for business," Miss Anne said.

"Goodness gracious, no," Miss Amy said. "Anne couldn't sleep, and we were both so anxious about poor Laura Stark. Is there any news, Mr. Burton?"

"None," I said.

"Captain Folwell asked us so many questions about her," Miss Anne said. "Such a sweet girl. It isn't often Amy and I get to make friends with young people."

"What kind of questions did Captain Folwell ask you?"

"Oh, about her friends," Miss Anne said.

"The people she knew well," Miss Amy said.

"Who did she know well?" I asked.

Miss Amy gave me an arch smile. Miss Anne batted her

eyelashes at me. "Well, there was you, of course," they said, in chorus.

"I was just a fan," I said. "I enjoyed her piano."

"Oh, my!" Miss Amy said.

"She was certainly curious about you," Miss Anne said.

At some other time I would have been delighted to pursue that tack, but right then I was still toying with the question of who could have persuaded Laura to walk out of my cottage and into the arms of a kidnapper. I tried to explain that to the Quigley sisters.

"Of course everybody crowded around her in the bar when she was doing her stuff at the piano," I said, "but I hadn't noticed anyone special."

"Except you!" Miss Amy said.

"'I think he's my number one fan,' she told us," Miss Anne said.

"I never saw her circulating around the inn with anyone in the daytime," I said.

"She was so involved with the music she was writing," Miss Amy said.

"She had dreams of a Broadway musical," Miss Anne said.

"She's been to your house, hasn't she?" I asked.

"Twice," Miss Amy said.

"Once for supper and once for a Sunday dinner," Miss Anne said.

"You'd known her from somewhere else?" Laura had been at the Red Cardinal for about a month.

"No," Miss Amy said. "Dick Carson heard her play at some café in Poughkeepsie—."

"A night club, not a café, Miss Anne said.

"He was so impressed he engaged her to come here and play through Labor Day," Miss Amy said.

"She didn't know anybody."

"She wandered into the shop the first morning she was here."

"We introduced ourselves."

"She was all alone so we invited her for supper."

"She didn't know anyone in Camden—away from the inn?" I asked, trying to break up the avalanche.

"She never mentioned anyone," Miss Anne said.

"I'm sure she would have—if there'd been anyone," Miss Amy said.

I stood there, looking around at the crowded shelves of the gift shop.

"Anne and I were wondering," Miss Amy said.

"If there is anything at all we can do," Miss Anne said.

"To be of help to Miss Walton," Miss Amy said.

"I guess she wants the same thing as the rest of us," I said. "Laura back in one piece. I have a theory that she's being held somewhere close by, perhaps on the inn grounds somewhere. The troopers have searched every square inch of the place, and yet somehow I keep thinking—."

"The book?" Miss Amy said to Miss Anne.

"The book!" Miss Anne said.

Miss Amy made her way through their incredible collection of merchandise to the rear end of the shop. She came back after a moment carrying a dust-covered book, bound in some kind of imitation red leather.

"It was privately printed," Miss Anne said, watching Miss Amy clean the dust away with a cloth she produced from behind the counter.

"Miss Millicent Hawthorne," Miss Amy said. "She was some sort of Camden town historian until just before the War. She wrote a history of the town and the surrounding villages. And she wrote this one about the Red Cardinal Inn. I guess it's the most important historical landmark in the community, going back before the Revolutionary War." She handed me the book.

It appeared that Miss Millicent Hawthorne hadn't been able to find a publisher for her work, and she'd had it privately printed. It was obviously a work of love, loaded with photographs and artists' drawings.

"The inn was originally just a one-room tavern," Miss Amy said. "You'll see drawings of it there in the beginning. Anne and I think that was what is the present bar. After that cellars were dug, wings were added, the second and third floors were built on top of that. In two hundred years it grew from one room to the great mansion you see here now. About 1910, part of it burned down and they remodeled it in the Tudor style it is now. I think there are drawings or photographs of every addition as it was built."

"Except the cottages at the rear," Miss Anne said. "They came after Miss Hawthorne's time, I guess, and anyway they aren't part of the main building."

"If there's any place the troopers overlooked you should find it accounted for in this book, Mr. Burton," Miss Amy said.

Well, I thought, bitterly, I had reading matter to occupy me while Laura waited for her kidnappers to decide her fate. Not having any notion of how to act was getting to me, but good.

I asked the two obliging old gals to keep an eye open for Chips and I went back across the lobby, carrying my book with me, and down the stairs to the catacombs. I suddenly needed a cup of coffee in the worst way. It was six o'clock. We had four hours until the deadline the kidnappers had given us—and no sensible scheme for using the time.

The aroma of Mrs. Kramer's fresh baking titilated my appetite. She was stacking trays of breads, rolls, coffee cakes, and other delights on the narrow shelves of a wagon on wheels.

"Steal a couple?" I asked her, indicating a tempting tray of blueberry muffins.

She made a gesture that indicated "be my guest." Fritz Schlee, the king of the kitchen, had a radio blasting out rock music that made normal conversation impossible. I shouted at Mrs. Kramer.

"Any sign of Chips?"

She shook her head.

I crossed the kitchen and took a coffee cup out of the racks of clean dishes and went over to one of the big steel coffee urns. Fritz grinned at me from where he was broiling strips of bacon. I took a plate and a pat of butter for my muffins and sat down at the corner of one of the long serving tables. I could see Chips' breakfast in the warming oven where Mrs. Kramer had put it some time ago. It didn't look very appetizing anymore.

I buttered a muffin and opened Miss Millicent Hawthorne's *The Red Cardinal Inn.* The lady had been no stylist as a writer, but she'd organized her material, particularly the drawings and photographs, so that the growth of the inn from a one-room village pub, to a stagecoach stop during the Revolution, to the industrial revolution headed by Henry Ford and his Model-T cars that put the general public on the roads, to its present status as a first-class country inn. I say "present," but Miss Hawthorne had evidently run out of gas or died about the beginning of World War II. As the gift shop gals had told me there were no pictures of the cottages out back. There had been a lush looking vegetable garden where they now stood.

One thing puzzled me as I thumbed through the book. There were maybe a dozen drawings and photos of "the north end of the building on the road to Greenville." The second story to the inn had been added about the time of Andrew Jackson. There was an outside stairway leading from the ground level to that second floor. After the fire in 1910, during William Howard Taft's presidency, when it had been remodeled, a third floor had been added, and that outside stairway had been extended up, like the back stroke of a capital Z. All the pictures of that north end showed that outside staircase, the last of them dated in 1937. I supposed its purpose had been to act as a fire-escape. It wasn't there now, hadn't been there when I first saw the hotel some fifteen years ago.

I finished a muffin, sipped my very excellent coffee, and carried the book over to Fritz.

"You ever see this book?" I shouted at him.

He nodded as he placed some fresh strips of bacon on his broiler pan.

"Was this staircase ever here in your time?" I asked him, pointing to the 1937 photograph.

He shook his head. "They put modern escape ladders in all the rooms," he shouted back. "Didn't need it anymore. Then they built on the third floor sundeck."

The present facade of the north end came into focus in my mind. Opening off the third-floor corridor was a wide porch, surrounded by a white rail fence. In the summertime there were deck chairs set up out there, some of them with colored umbrellas over them. It was a place for sunbathing or just to sit and enjoy the gorgeous view of meadows and rolling hills. Underneath the deck was just the windowless red clapboarding from ground level to the floor of the deck.

"They tore off the staircase," I suggested.

Fritz grinned at me. "Just walled it in," Fritz said. "He didn't use it in your time?"

"Who didn't use what?"

"Your boss. They say he used to use that walled-in stairway to get to his lady when she first moved in here. Before my time."

"You mean there's a concealed way up to the Duchess's apartment?"

"I think it's boarded up at both ends," he said. "It's never been used since I've been here and that's twenty years."

"Troopers look there?" I asked him.

His smile faded. "I don't think so. There's a floor plan of the basement I showed them. The old stairway isn't marked on it because in a sense it isn't there. Isn't there. Isn't used. Like I said, I think it's boarded up."

"But you didn't mention it to Captain Folwell?"

"Why should I? I hadn't thought about it in a long time till you just brought it up."

I'm not sure I can tell you what I was thinking about it at that moment. You couldn't hide a girl there and keep her there for hours and hours—if she were alive. But Mr. X's dead body could have been hidden there for two days since nobody had thought to look there. And Laura, if they'd known they could never set her free.

"I'd like to have a look at it," I said.

"You can't, it's boarded up!" Fritz said.

"Let's make sure," I said.

"You'll have to do your own snooping," Fritz said. "I've got breakfast to get for an inn full of guests. It's at the very end of the tunnel. You'll see the boards they put up across the old exit."

I started away, leaving my book and my coffee.

"You'll need a flashlight," Fritz called after me. "Tool shop."

I knew where the tool shop was and I found the light switch just inside the door. The tool shop is Chips' domain and it was neat and orderly as you might expect. I spotted a flashlight hanging in a clamp on the wall and I took it.

I walked down the tunnel to the very end and found myself facing a blank stone wall. Boarded up, Fritz had said. I swung the flash around and saw what I was looking for. At right angle to the rear wall was a boarded section—the corner of the building, I realized. It stood slightly ajar, like a door. It was a door, although it wasn't outlined by any sort of frame; just planks nailed together that swung outward if you knew about them. There was no handle or knob.

I reached out and pulled it open wider. There was the boarded-up stairway that years ago had been a fire escape. It was pitch dark up those stairs. Those nervous hackles were rising on my neck. Someone had used this entrance quite recently. Chips? He would know about it.

I started up, spraying the light around ahead of me. Then I saw it—a body sprawled, head downward, on the stairs. A man. I bent down and played the light full on his face. It was Mr. Arthur Townsend, the vacationing gent from Summit, New Jersey. There was a bullet hole in the center of his forehead.

Two

With only the flashlight to see by I had been convinced, in the moment before I identified Arthur Townsend, that I was looking at Chips. It would have explained his abandoning his breakfast, his absence for the last hour. If anyone knew about the walled-in staircase it would certainly have been Chips.

It was with a sense of personal relief that I searched for a pulse beat at Townsend's throat. I knew I wasn't going to feel anything. I know a gunshot wound when I see it, and this one could not have been less than fatal There were two instant questions as I started back down the stairway for help. What was a casual, transient traveler doing in the walled-in staircase at the Red Cardinal and who could have objected to it enough to kill him?

I told Fritz, on the fly, what I had found and went looking for Dick Carson. Dick was still asleep in the armchair in his cottage sitting room, the Duchess's casette player on the table in front of him. I don't think he quite believed what I was telling him as he tried to pull himself together.

"What the hell were you doing there, Dan?" he asked me.

I told him about the Quigley sisters' book. "Trying to find someplace we hadn't looked for Laura," I said.

He was already dialing the state police number and I knew that the Red Cardinal was about to be turned inside-out for the third time in less than thirty hours.

My first thought after that was for the Duchess. That

walled-in staircase passed just behind the bedroom of her second-floor suite. According to Fritz, Wilfred Krider had used it as a way to get to his love in the old days. I must have awakened half the hotel as I pounded on the door to her jumble room, trying to attract her attention, calling out to her. This time she was wearing a terrycloth robe and some kind of a cap when she finally opened up.

"Damn it, Daniel, is there no time at all for any peace and quiet?" she demanded to know.

"Are you all right?" I asked her.

"Everything is relative," she said. "I'm not all right if you consider a little rest is important after all that's happened here."

"More has happened," I said. "There's a walled-up staircase that leads to your bedroom. Show me where it is."

"Daniel, that staircase hasn't been used for twenty-five years!" she said. "More than that, I think."

"It's been used tonight. There's a dead man not ten feet away from the wall of your bedroom."

She reached out to steady herself on the back of her throne-chair. "Who, Daniel?"

"A man named Townsend, staying here with his wife. They were in the bar last night when you spotted Mr. X in the pool. They were there when Folwell questioned us all."

"Dead you say?" All the natural color had faded from her face.

"Shot smack between the eyes," I said. "You hear a gunshot?"

"Good lord, no!" she said. "When?"

"I don't know—yet," I said. "We haven't had any chance to check out. I found him about fifteen minutes ago." I explained to her about Millicent Hawthorne's history of the inn, and how I'd gone to explore the staircase as a possible hiding place for the kidnapped Laura. "Show me where the staircase comes into your bedroom, Duchess."

She walked unsteadily through her piles of junk to the

bedroom. Morning sunlight streamed through the windows. She stood facing her dressing table with its theatrically lighted mirror. She pointed.

"Behind that," she said.

I was a cop again. Before I tried to move the table I examined the wall-to-wall carpet on which it rested. There were deep indentations where the table had rested, probably for years. If it had been moved at all, it had probably been only briefly out of position for Mildred, the maid, to vacuum under it. The bedroom, contrary to the jumble room, was spotlessly clean. I lifted the table away, leaving the mirror hanging where it was. What was revealed was the lower half of a window that had been covered when the north end of the building had been boarded up. The window opened onto the old fire escape. It was open now, the glass panes thick with dust and grime. It had not been Mildred's job to clean there. Light came up the old stairway now and there were excited voices. Dick Carson and other help had located Arthur Townsend.

"Dick!" I called down. "All okay up here."

"Thank God," Dick called back. "The Duchess hear anything, see anything?"

I glanced at her. She looked bewildered. She shook her head, slowly.

"Nothing," I called back to Dick.

From outside the wail of a siren reached us. Captain Folwell was on his way to the Red Cardinal for the third time in thirty hours.

Nothing was meant to be simple for the trooper captain. Mrs. Townsend, Caroline Townsend, was asleep when Folwell roused her. Perhaps he was a little abrupt with the news, because the lady screamed and went into shock. She hadn't seemed to be disturbed that her husband wasn't in the other twin bed, but the news of his death shook her loose from her moorings. An emergency call was put in for Dr. Chance who, it turned out, was on his way to cover Townsend's killing as the town's medical officer.

Sergeant Lacey threw Folwell his next curve. Townsend turned out not to be Townsend! That is to say, the identification on the body indicated that the man who had called himself Townsend registered at the inn as Townsend, was actually someone named Kenneth Lukens, also from Summit, New Jersey. His driver's license, four credit cards, and some blank checks in his wallet all made it clear that the dead man was Kenneth Lukens.

Car keys opened the glove compartment of the little MG convertible the couple were driving, and there they found the car registration. According to that, the car belonged to Arthur Townsend.

"When you run an inn you don't ask for birth certificates or a marriage license when a strange couple registers," Dick Carson told Folwell. He had never seen the couple who had registered as Mr. and Mrs. Townsend before. He'd had no reason to question them.

"Looks like Mrs. Townsend was having a ball with a Summit neighbor, using her husband's car," Dick suggested.

"No wonder she went into shock," Folwell muttered.

Whoever he was the man was very dead, and there were no leads so far to that. Neither Fritz Schlee nor Mrs. Kramer in the catacombs admitted to ever seeing the dead man before, which meant only that Townsend—or Lukens—hadn't made a habit of wandering around in the kitchen area. Guests never got to the kitchen unless they were taken on a guided tour for some reason. Lukens—or Townsend—hadn't been.

It took about a half an hour for Folwell to straighten out the matter of identity in a phone call to the Summit police. Both Arthur Townsend and Kenneth Lukens were well-known residents of the New Jersey town. Arthur Townsend was a bachelor, in the insurance business in Summit, and at the present on a holiday somewhere in Europe. The MG convertible was his. Townsend's sister, Caroline, was married to Kenneth Lukens. And here came the crusher as far as we were concerned. Kenneth Lukens was a vice-president of Krider Industries in New York.

"No matter where you turn it comes up Krider," Folwell said. "What was the bastard doing here using his brother-in-law's name?"

"What was he doing in that walled-in staircase leading to the Duchess's bedroom?" I asked. "And where the hell is Chips?"

I had a vision of Chips getting his breakfast in the kitchen, spotting Kenneth Lukens on his way down the tunnel in the catacombs, going after him—and then what?

It was after seven when we began to try to put those pieces together. Dr. Chance was working over Caroline Townsend Lukens. That's who she was. A quick search of the handbag in her room revealed her own driver's license.

"Convertibles are scarce as hen's teeth these days," Dick Carson said. "They borrowed it while her brother was in Europe to use on their vacation."

"Nobody connected with Krider Industries comes to Camden on a vacation," Folwell muttered. "They come here for trouble. Where is Chips?"

A couple of hours had passed since Chips had cooked his breakfast and then walked away from it before the first piece of toast, the first strip of bacon was tasted. It was still sitting downstairs in the warming oven. By now most of the kitchen and house staff were on their jobs. No one, coming on fresh, had seen him.

Asking yourself when you had last seen Chips in the Red Cardinal was like asking yourself when you had last seen the mail box in the lobby or the life-sized model of a Revolutionary War soldier who guarded the entrance to the gift shop. You had always just seen Chips somewhere. Except nobody remembered seeing him now since—when? He and I had gone to look in Laura's room after we'd had word from the kidnapper. He'd gone on to look for her while I'd checked out on the Duchess. Mrs. Kramer had seen him in the catacombs around five o'clock, getting his breakfast. Mrs. Kramer had been too busy with her baking to pay attention to Chips' leaving.

"You know why he slept in the inn the last three nights instead of his own bed?" I asked Dick. "He told Dominic 'because of the trouble in the inn.' We didn't know we had any trouble till one o'clock Thursday morning."

"I didn't know he was staying in the main building," Dick said.

"Wouldn't he ask you for permission?" Folwell asked. "Does the help just sleep around anywhere they want?"

Dick gave us a wry smile. "Chips wouldn't have to ask," he said. "I might have to ask him if I wanted him to move, but Chips was free to do what he pleased. He had a reason, so he did it."

"He's just a mop-man, isn't he?" Folwell asked.

"Oh, he's a mop-man," Dick said. "He's also a repair man, a Mr. Fix-it, a fill-in for any job on the lot. If he didn't like the looks of some guest, or the way some night job was being done, he wouldn't bother me with it till he was certain of his facts. I would have expected him to move into the main building after the murder of Mr. X. I have no notion why he changed beds two days before that. But he had a reason that was healthy for the inn, you can count on that."

"He was looking for Laura that last time I saw him," I said.

"Well, we know she isn't being held anywhere around here," Folwell said.

"We don't know any such thing," I said. "You've searched every place you thought of, but not every place. You didn't know that walled-in staircase existed."

"Well, she isn't there!" Folwell said. "Nor any sign that she's ever been there."

"I knew about the staircase," Dick said. "It's been boarded up for years. It never occurred to me—."

"What about other places that haven't occurred to you, chum?" I said.

"Right now I'm interested in the person who shot this Kenneth Lukens," Folwell said.

"Good for you," I said. I was burning a little. "I'm interested in finding a girl who may get her throat cut if we don't locate her in time."

I guess if I'd been in Folwell's boots I'd have been irritated by me. "Look, Burton, you've asked me to believe one set of facts and I'm working on them. You've asked me to believe that the man we call Mr. X came here ten years ago to kill Wilfred Krider. You don't know that for a fact. He was guilty of breaking and entering back then and, as a bodyguard, you shot him. Maybe he wasn't here then to kill Krider at all. Maybe he was here to look for this incriminating tape you're talking about now. Had you thought of that?"

The truth was I hadn't. The Old Man was sure Mr. X. was here to kill him—treachery within the ranks of Krider Industries. If Folwell, not-so-dumb cop, had hit on it, the picture was suddenly painted in different colors. Ten years ago, Mr. X had come to Camden looking for the tape. Who would have it then? The Old Man, of course. Where would he look for it? At *Hilltop* on Camden Mountain. Where else? He nearly got himself killed in the attempt, but some ally with him or already located in Camden, got him away.

Ten years later, Krider is long dead, but Mr. X comes back. Still looking for the tape? Your guess is as good as mine. He goes looking for it in a place where the old man could be presumed to have left it, in the care of his lady, the Duchess, or his bodyguard, me. Now, however, there is a new character in the plot, someone who knows Mr. X by sight and why he has come back. He shoots Mr. X, hides his body for two days, and then dumps it in the pool. This new character either has the tape or knows who has it.

Now comes another new character on the scene, "Mr. Arthur Townsend" of Summit, New Jersey. Except he isn't Arthur Townsend, but Kenneth Lukens, a vice-president of Krider Industries. Why does he come to Camden and the Red Cardinal under an assumed name?

"It's possible that not a damned word of any of this is true," Folwell said. "I mean, Mr. X may have nothing on earth to do with Krider Industries. Lukens does. He is here, under a false name when X's body is dumped in the pool. He is here the next day when Laura Stark is kidnapped from your house. He is here this morning, staying longer than his original reservation suggested he would stay, prowling around in a boarded-up stairway that leads to Miss Walton's bedroom. We know damned well he isn't an archeologist interested in old buildings. He's a vice-president of Krider. Our killer is still here somewhere, tracks Lukens down, shoots him. If any of this dream-up about a tape is true, I have to believe Lukens was looking for it, just as X was looking for it. And let's go just one step further with it, Burton. If the tape exists, if it isn't something Mark Stone dreamed up and persuaded you to believe, if it's for real, then I have to assume that the person or persons who kidnapped Laura Stark are on the same team as X was, as Lukens was; a team out to find an incriminating tape. You and Miss Walton are presumed to be the most likely guardians of that tape. Her room is searched. Your house is searched. Lukens is in a secret passage on his way to her room to make a second search."

"And the killer is right here, in my hotel, watching every move Lukens might make," Dick Carson said.

The vision of Chips, preparing his breakfast in the catacombs, persisted. He sees Lukens slip into the kitchen area and head down the tunnel. He puts aside his breakfast and follows. And then?

"The girl is kidnapped to force your hand, or Miss Walton's," Folwell said. "You both say you don't have the tape."

"I don't have it," I said. "I never heard of it till Stone suggested it to me on the phone."

"And Miss Walton?"

"She swears she hasn't got it, never heard of it."

Folwell drew a deep, weary breath. "You have a hot line to this man Stone," he said. "A vice-president of his company has been murdered. It's time he got into the act, don't you think?"

"I can try," I said. Laura was, however, still my main concern. "Are you thinking that Lukens and Company may have taken the girl?"

"If any of this makes any sense, that makes sense," Folwell said. He glanced at his watch. "There are a couple of hours before the kidnappers are supposed to contact you. If it was Lukens he isn't going to call, you know. Try to contact Stone and get him here. While you're doing that, I think it's time Dr. Chance got Mrs. Lukens in shape to talk."

I looked at Dick Carson. "Find Chips," I said. "He's got to be somewhere around, and I have a hunch he saw something, knows something. He was in the kitchen about the time Lukens must have found his way to the old stairway."

I went to the private line in Dick Carson's office and dialed Stone's number. That ever-polite secretary answered after a few rings.

"I'm sorry, Mr. Burton, I can't connect you with Mr. Stone."

"You know where he is?"

"I'm afraid I couldn't tell you that if I did know," she said. It was a way of answering my question.

"When you can get in touch with him," I said, "tell him that Kenneth Lukens, a vice-president of your company, has been murdered here in Camden."

"Oh no!" the polite secretary said.

I had left the Duchess with her privacy shattered. Troopers had barged into her bedroom through the old window walled in behind her dressing table. They searched the old window for finger prints. They insisted the dead Mr. Lukens could only have gotten into the walled-in stairway through the Duchess's bedroom. That is an old-time police technique. You think you have a suspect, no matter how far-fetched, and you try to make square facts fit into a round hole. The old lady remembered Lukens as Arthur Townsend. He'd been one of the small group in the bar when she saw the man in the pool. She'd had no conversation with Lukens or his wife, she insisted, beyond something profound like "What an awful thing!" She hadn't seen either of the Lukenses since that first murder; she hadn't followed her regular routines since then, couldn't remember that she'd even spoken to them or noticed them the next night when she'd spent some time in the President's Room—lounge, to you. She'd had no interest in the Townsends-or-Lukenses. She was adamant on this. She had no reason to know that Lukens had any connection with Krider Industries and Wilfred Krider had never discussed corporate business or personnel. She and the Old Man had never had any social contacts with any Krider people. The only two people with Krider connections she had ever met in all the years of her life with Wilfred Krider were Mark Stone, head of Krider security, who'd appeared on the scene at the time of Mr. X's attempt on the Old Man's life, and Josh Krider, the Old Man's grandson, who had made a nasty drunken scene over her in the President's Room one night a couple of years ago.

"It was fortunate for that young man that Will was dead," the Duchess said.

I remember that scene very well. I walked in on it in the middle of a name calling outrage—"my grandfather's doxy—a ninety-year-old sex object—a cheap tart all her life." Chips was in process of a rather tough effort to kick that turkey out on his ear. I was delighted to be able to lend him a hand. That was the only time I'd ever laid hands on Josh until yesterday morning. I'd dreamed of it more than once, however.

I was standing in the doorway of the jumble room when the Duchess handed that information to Sergeant Belter who was conducting what he thought of as an interrogation.

"Only two people, eh?" he said. "You knew Dan Burton, didn't you?"

She looked at me, and her eyes were bright. She wasn't caving at all. "Of course I know Daniel," she said. "Know him, and am very fond of him. But he has nothing to do with Krider Industries and never has had. He was Will Krider's personal friend and bodyguard, and he has been my friend and someone I could count on ever since Will died."

"And well-paid to do the job," Belter said.

"I like to think I could have counted on him whether Will had a financial arrangement with him or not," the Duchess said.

I walked into the room. "She could and can," I said. "What the hell are you trying to do, Belter? Make a case by just shooting off your mouth? There's a killer wandering around here somewhere and you're taking time out to turn the heat on a ninety-year-old woman!"

"Ninety-four to be exact," the Duchess said. She looked very tall, and straight, with a kind of marvelous dignity.

Belter didn't enjoy being told off. "Just come into the bedroom, both of you," he said.

The dressing table was still pulled away from the wall, and behind it was the old lower half of the window, open. I could still hear voices coming up from below.

"Those guys aren't shouting down there," Belter said. "You hear them, Burton?"

"I hear them."

"Everyone talks about this staircase being boarded up," he said. "Well, it isn't boarded up on the inside end; never has been. If there was something going on in that stairway area you could hear it in this room. You couldn't shoot off a cap pistol in there and not hear it in this room. Is there anything wrong with your hearing, Miss Walton?"

The Duchess gave him a cold look. "Nothing whatever," she said.

"And you haven't left these rooms all night?"

"I haven't left them, but I haven't been alone very much," she said. "I might remark in passing, Sergeant, there was a time when Wilfred Krider used that old stairway as a way to visit me here in my rooms. That was before your time, Daniel. No matter how quietly Will came, I could always hear him from the moment he started up from the bottom." She looked away, down that long road to the past. "Of course, in those days, I was listening for him. But I'm trying to back you up, Sergeant. That stairway is like a well. You could hear a pebble drop in the bottom of it. Nobody could have fired a gun in there without my hearing it."

"This character was found in there, dead, with a bullet hole in his forehead," Belter said.

"Then I suggest he was shot somewhere else and his body moved there."

"Oh for Pete's sake, Miss Walton—excuse me!" Belter exploded. "What have we got, some kind of body-moving concern? The first guy was shot, kept hidden for two days, then dragged around and dumped in the pool. Now you suggest this Lukens was shot somewhere else and his body lugged into that stairwell! There are only two ways he could be gotten in there, Miss Walton. Through that window in your wall, or through the kitchen area where there's someone on duty almost around the clock."

"Well, he certainly wasn't carried through here," the Duchess said.

Somebody was knocking on the jumble room door and I went to see who it was. Captain Folwell and Dick Carson were waiting. The trooper captain had his jaw set in a kind of determined fashion.

"Well, at least we know that we're dealing with one killer and not a gang of lunatics," he said. "We'll have ballistics experts in Hartford double check for us, but my people are satisfied that Mr. X and Lukens were killed by the same gun. Same rifling, same eccentricities."

"Which means the killer has been hanging around here since Monday," Dick Carson said.

"So who's next?" I said.

Folwell gave me a sharp look. "The kidnapper seems to think you and/or Miss Walton have what he wants, or can produce it for him," he said. "If the kidnapper is also the murderer, I'd say you and Miss Walton could be on his list. That's why I'm here. I think you both need a little extra protection for a while."

Sergeant Belter gave me a dirty look. "Burton carries a gun," he said. "I'd feel a hell of a lot better if we checked it out in the ballistics barrel."

The "ballistics barrel" is a container full of cotton, or wool, or some soft junk into which you can fire a bullet without marking it up.

"If I have a job these days," I said, "it's looking out for Miss Walton. I'll turn over my gun to you if you'll give me another one till I get it back."

"I'll give you a trooper to hold your hand," Folwell said. He reached out for me to pass him my gun. I sure as hell didn't want to give it up, but I did. "You reached your friend Stone?" he asked.

"No, but I left a message for him. It ought to bring him when he gets it. How about we close up the wall in Miss Walton's bedroom. I'm apt to bushwhack anybody who tries to come up here that way."

"Close it up," Folwell said, and turned away, taking my gun with him. I was suddenly a safer target than I'd been two minutes ago.

The two troopers and Dick Carson left us. I went into the bedroom and nearly broke my back trying to get that old window in the wall closed. I don't think it had been moved up or down for years. I finally made it. Then I shoved the dressing table back into place and the room looked normal again.

The Duchess had dropped down in her throne chair in the jumble room, her tinted eyelids lowered, her head thrown back against the chair's high back. There was still great beauty in that profile; no double chins, no sagging wartles. She would still have been a great subject for a sculptor's chisel. I found myself thinking of her long love affair with the Old Man. She must have been so very beautiful, the kind of woman a man would be proud to show off, to let the world know that she belonged to him. Yet he had kept her virtually hidden in back streets and in this quiet country inn for half a lifetime.

I glanced at her picture gallery on the wall behind her throne, more than a dozen warmly autographed pictures of the most romantic male stage and screen stars of fifty years ago, the Barrymores, Leslie Howard, Charles Boyer, Basil Sydney. She must have enjoyed the admiration she'd had from all of them in her days on the stage, and yet she'd cared so much for the Old Man, the Napoleon of Krider Industries, that she'd given all that up to please him. And herself, no doubt. Krider evidently hadn't objected to having those pictures on the wall. Perhaps they reminded him of how good his competition had been, and how good he must have been to leave them all taking his dust.

"Tell me, darlin'," I said, "was Chips one of the people who's been in and out of your rooms tonight?"

She opened her eyes to look at me. "Didn't he come here with you—early on?"

"But since then?"

She shook her head, slowly.

"He was getting his breakfast in the kitchen about three hours ago when something interrupted him," I said. "He never came back for that breakfast and nobody seems to know where he is."

"Dear Chips," she said, apparently not disturbed by the

news. "A nice, kind, gentle man who lost his way and wound up here at the inn, far off his original goal. You knew that Will got him his job here, didn't you?"

I tried to recall what Dick Carson had told me about hiring Chips. Someone had suggested to him that the way to get a mop man who wouldn't steal his liquor was to hire a cured alcoholic. Had that someone been Krider?

"Did you know that before I met Will he'd had a drinking problem?" the Duchess asked.

I hadn't known. It didn't seem likely, remembering him. He was a man of such enormous control as I knew him.

"Will had deep sympathy for men who had the same problem," the Duchess said. "Chips was a teacher in Wadsworth Academy, the boys' school just north of Camden, you know. There was some kind of scandal about another teacher's wife—and booze. Will heard about it, and I think he secretly did what he could to help Chips. Chips won his own battle after a while and Will managed to get him his job here with Richard Carson. It wasn't Chips' kind of life, but he was eternally grateful to Will. I think he tried to show it by being always helpful, and protective, and kind to me. There were long stretches, when Will was away on business, when Chips was the only person I had to talk to. He is a cultivated, highly educated man, you know."

"I don't feel easy about him," I said. "He could be in some kind of trouble."

"I can't think of anyone better able to face trouble head on than Chips," she said. "You know, Daniel, you're a very tough man when action is called for. That's why Will counted on you. But Chips can outthink the cleverest schemer. He's not likely to be caught off guard if there is trouble around. I'm very lucky to have had you both to look out for me all this time. You've both helped to make me feel so safe—after Will left."

I appreciated the flattery but it didn't make me feel better about Chips. If he'd been that close to Krider he could well be at the very center of what was going on here.

Three

Sent to hold my hand was an absurdly young-looking trooper named Chapman.

"I'm just supposed to hang around with you until they decide you're safe," he said. He looked at the Duchess as though he might be viewing the contents of King Tut's tomb. I guess he'd never seen her before. "I'm supposed to check back with the Captain." He was looking around for a telephone.

There was no telephone in the Duchess's rooms. The Old Man, in the days when he visited here, had wanted no way for the outside world to interrupt his pleasures. After he had jogged his last mile I'd urged the Duchess to have one installed, connected with the switchboard. She might need help; it would simplify keeping in touch with her. She wouldn't hear of it. Will hadn't wanted one and she wasn't changing anything, except to increase her collection of clippings and magazines and books about the Old Man. Running up and down the stairs from the lobby to check on her had helped to keep my waistline down.

A telephone was beginning to assume a special importance to me. In about an hour and a half we could be hearing from the kidnappers. Their call had come through the switchboard the first time. I needed to be somewhere I could answer promptly.

Chapman's orders were to stay with me, but I managed to talk him out of it. I didn't want the Duchess left alone; I wouldn't be going out of the inn, which must be awake and very much alive by now with a new murder to buzz over; I would go and stay with Folwell till the phone call came. I guess I made it sound logical.

I'm not sure the Duchess was happy about it. She trusted me. She must have thought of Chapman as a child. I promised to get back to her as soon as anything broke.

"Lie down and get some rest," I told her. "The trooper will stand guard out here." I thought the nude painting in the bedroom might really leave him gaping.

I was right about the state of things in the inn. The word about Lukens had spread and people were churning between the lobby and the dining room. I was starting to look around for Folwell when I saw one of the Quigley sisters beckoning to me from the gift shop entrance.

It was Miss Amy. "How awful!" she said.

Miss Anne was right behind her. "We thought his name was Townsend. He spent some time in the shop yesterday morning."

"He bought a copy of the book," Miss Amy said.

Hello, I thought. "The book about the inn?"

"The one we gave you to look at," Miss Anne said. "We keep copies of it to sell to guests."

"He was curious about the Red Cardinal's history?" I asked.

"Like everyone else," Miss Amy said, "he was wondering where the body of that first dead man could have been hidden for two days before it was dumped in the pool."

"Everybody becomes a detective when there's a crime," Miss Anne said.

"You tell Captain Folwell this?"

"Nobody's come to ask us anything so far," Miss Amy said.

"Not that we know anything," Miss Anne said.

I turned to go. "You still haven't seen Chips?"

"No." Miss Amy said. "Not a sight of him."

"He usually checks with us before we open up in the morning, but not today," Miss Anne said.

Miss Amy gestured toward the freshly baked breads and cookies and cakes Mrs. Kramer had brought up from the catacombs. "We'd be glad to save you something, Mr. Burton, if you'd care to make a choice."

"I don't think I'll have much appetite for a while," I said. "But thanks."

Folwell didn't seem to be anywhere around on the ground floor and I guessed he must be trying to talk to Lukens' wife. The desk told me she was in 306—the third floor. I trudged up there and knocked. Sergeant Lacey opened the door to me.

"Something he needs to know while he's here," I said.

From where I stood I could see the bureau in the room, and resting on top of it was the red leather-bound copy of Millicent Hawthorne's *The Red Cardinal Inn.*

Folwell and Dick Carson were with the lady, who was propped up against pillows on her bed. Dr. Chance had evidently gotten her in shape to talk. He was gone.

I took Folwell aside and told him about the book. It seemed apparent Lukens hadn't just stumbled on the walled-in staircase by accident. Like me, having looked through Millicent Hawthorne's book, he'd known where to look for it.

However genuine her shock and grief had been—and were—Caroline Townsend Lukens seemed prepared to face the enemy. She was one of those people, I suspected, who considers everyone who doesn't belong to a small, closed circle of intimate friends and family to be the opposition. If she hadn't been so obviously braced aginst Folwell's interrogation I might have felt some sympathy for her. Whatever her husband had been up to, he hadn't expected to be plugged between the eyes. Nor had she expected it. Now she was going to have to field some rather awkward questions. She must have been asleep when they brought her the news. She'd had no chance to dress or prepare herself in a female way for this male invasion. The adjoining twin bed, her husband's, had not been slept in. She was a pleasant-enough-looking woman in her late forties. I'd thought that when I saw her in the bar the night Mr. X was discovered in the pool. Now, sitting up in bed, wearing a pale blue dressing gown over pajamas, sheet drawn up over a fairly ample bosom, her face was set in hard, defensive lines.

I didn't know how far Folwell had got with his questions before I appeared. There were things I wanted answered. Why had Lukens bought the book? Why had he been snooping around the hidden areas of the inn instead of coming to bed? Had she been worried about him, or had she not expected him to show up? Folwell must have asked some of those questions. I could only guess what her answers had been as he went on with his questions.

"I think you know Dan Burton," Folwell said.

She nodded. "He was in the bar when they discovered the body in the pool," she said.

"Your husband probably told you that Burton worked for his company at one time."

"Not true," I said. "I never worked for Krider Industries. I worked for Wilfred Krider."

"The same thing," Folwell said. "Wilfred Krider *was* Krider Industries."

"Not the same thing. I worked for him, not the company."

"Whatever. Did your husband mention that to you, Mrs. Lukens?"

"No," she said. "I had no idea."

Folwell was fighting his own impatience. "I find it hard to believe, Mrs. Lukens, that you and your husband would come here to the Red Cardinal Inn, register under a false name, stay longer than you'd intended after the murder of X, and that you would go placidly to bed and sleep the sleep of the just while your husband goes searching the basement of the inn—and not know why he was here in Camden, why under your brother's name, the whole schmear."

She took a deep breath. "You're local, Captain Folwell," she said. "You know that when Wilfred Krider was alive,

Camden was a center of operations for Krider Industries. Wilfred Krider was the king, the tzar, the works. Wilfred Krider's estate has only just been probated. Ken had some questions about it. He wanted to make those inquiries without drawing attention to himself. My brother is in Europe on vacation. We borrowed his car because it's a convertible, no other reason. When he got here to the Red Cardinal, Ken suggested we register under Arthur's name. 'Townsend' wouldn't mean anything to anyone connected with Krider Industries."

I couldn't keep my mouth shut. "Wilfred Krider had a habit of taping all his business transactions," I said. "Did your husband tell you he was looking for one of those tapes?"

There was an almost imperceptible flicker of her eyelids. Cop-trained, my instinct told me I was about to be thrown a curve.

"He never mentioned a tape."

I expected Folwell to have me heaved out of the room, but he didn't. Instead, he looked at me as if he expected me to go on. That was alright with me.

"You and your husband both heard me identify X, the night we found him in the pool, as a paid hit-man who tried to kill Wilfred Krider ten years ago. What did your husband have to say about that?"

She hesitated for a moment. "He just said that Wilfred Krider had been involved in so many secret deals and under-the-table conspiracies there was no way to guess who might have hired what you call a hit-man to get him."

"Nothing in the world is going to bring your husband back, Mrs. Lukens," I said. "We know that the same gun killed your husband and X. That suggest the same man. I can tell you that Wilfred Krider thought that X, the hit-man, might have been hired by someone in his own company. If you know of any connection between your husband and X, tell us. If you know who your husband expected to see when he got to Camden, tell us. The kidnapper seems to feel that Miss Walton or I may have something he wants. We think it's a tape and we don't have it. If you can throw any light on all this, Mrs. Lukens, you might save another life. I can understand your protecting your husband's business secrets while he was alive. But now, if you know something and you don't pass it on to us, you can be an accessory to another murder."

It was a long speech for me, but I had seen those flickering eyelids. She was holding back something. Suddenly, she lowered her head and covered her face with her hands. Her voice faltered when she finally spoke.

"It *is* a tape," she said.

We all stood deathly still, afraid she might change her mind about going on.

"It has to do with some kind of a deal Ken and Wilfred Krider were involved in years ago," she said. "Gone and forgotten, I think. But Ken is—was—about to be elected president of Krider Industries. He—Ken—and Wilfred Krider were not friends toward the end of Krider's life. I don't know what they fell out over. But Ken told me Krider had this tape, and that if he ever came in line to succeed him, the tape could destroy him, and that Krider may have passed it on to someone to use. It never showed up in the settling of Krider's estate. Ken thought someone here in Camden might have it. He thought you, Mr. Burton, who had been Krider's bodyguard, or Miss Walton, who had been his mistress, or someone else here might have been trusted with it."

"Did he guess that X had been looking for it, too?"

"I think so."

"Did he search my cottage?"

She nodded. Then she lowered her hands from her face. "He was sorry about the dog, Mr. Burton. The animal attacked him."

"So tonight, through that book he picked up in the gift shop, he found a way to get to Miss Walton's room to search it?"

"Yes." It was a whisper.

"He never talked to me. He never talked to Miss Walton."

"He thought you were both too devoted to Krider to just turn over the tape to him. No point in talking to you. He had to find it on his own."

Something began to take shape for me. "When did you and your husband make the plan to stop off here in Camden on your vacation?" I asked.

She gave me a puzzled look. "It—it was rather abrupt," she said. "We had planned to leave Summit this weekend—tomorrow. On Tuesday evening he asked me if I could be ready to go the next morning. I could. We got here Wednesday afternoon, registering as Mr. and Mrs. Townsend. It was on the drive up that he told me about the tape and that he was going to try to find it. Nobody here would know him, except by name, which was the reason for the Townsend business."

I turned to Folwell. He was still leaving it to me.

"So he arranged to have the girl kidnapped, so Miss Walton or I would produce what he wanted?"

Caroline Lukens leaned back against her pillows and two large tears streamed down her cheeks. "The girl is safe, Mr. Burton," she said. "She wasn't kidnapped. She was bought."

I just stared at her.

"That night in the bar Ken saw how attached you seemed to be to the girl. Ken believed that every man—or woman—has a price. In Miss Stark's case he was right. She couldn't resist the Broadway musical that Ken dangled before her eyes. He got to her early in the morning after Mr. X had been found in the pool. I think you had gone up to Miss Walton's rooms. He gave her a big story about you—you were married with a wife and kids living in New York, and you'd been blackmailing him with a tape you had of your wife and him that could ruin him. Ken told her he had to get that tape away from you and he promised if she helped him he would finance a Broadway show with her music. They set you up. She came to sit in your cottage with you while you slept, and when you did sleep, she—she just walked away."

"Where is she?"

"I don't know. Ken gave her some money to stay under cover till you turned over what he wanted—the tape."

"Would he have kept his promise to her?" I asked, not wanting to believe her.

She shrugged. "He might have. Money wasn't important to Ken, only power. The tape stood in his way. They are electing a new president of Krider Industries next week. He was running out of time, Mr. Burton. He was desperate."

"So desperate he didn't try to buy me," I said. "I guess he knew I didn't have a price. But to keep a girl in danger—?"

I turned to Dick Carson. "So much for our dear little Laura," I said. "Maybe I should have offered her a few bucks instead of playing it for a romance."

"It wouldn't have been worth a Broadway musical," Dick said, giving me a sour smile.

Four

A cop's mind is trained to make everything fit one design. You get some leads to an answer and you try to make all the loose ends conform to those leads. I had a feeling that Caroline Lukens had told us the truth as far as she knew it. She had, I was sure, at least told us what her husband had told her. It explained Lukens' presence at the Red Cardinal under an alias. It explained why he had stayed on, been searching hidden places. It explained Laura Stark's "kidnapping." She hadn't been the victim of foul play. She had played me foul—she'd made a first-class sucker out of me. That story about my having a wife and kids probably really turned her off on me—after hearing that, she probably was only too glad to get back at me. Damn that Lukens. Why wouldn't she jump at the chance he offered her—her name up in lights on Broadway. The chance of a lifetime for her. It figured. It could take as much as a million bucks to get a Broadway musical ready to open. What kind of a percentage would he really have put up? To Lukens it was probably worth twenty times a million bucks, even more, to become the power figure in Krider Industries. His wife had said money didn't mean anything to him.

Watching the clock tick by, minute by minute that morning, eventually convinced us that the Laura story was probably the truth. By eleven o'clock, two hours after the banks had opened, there had been no promised call from the "kidnapper." He couldn't call because he was lying dead in the morgue at the trooper barracks. Laura was probably sitting somewhere, listening to a radio wondering what her next move should be. The murder of Kenneth Lukens was the big news story of the day. She knew now that her musical was fresh out of a backer. I felt rotten. It wasn't just that I had trusted her implicitly—I guess it was that she'd been so willing to think the worst of me. And so quick to throw me over for some tinsel and gold. Well, good-bye my sweet little baby chick—you wanted to fly away over the rainbow, but you took a fast nosedive into a mud puddle. That wasn't really the way I'd wanted it to end.

Unfortunately, from Folwell's point of view and mine, Caroline Lukens' story left out the one thing we needed to know most of all. Who had pulled the trigger on the gun that had killed Mr. X and Kenneth Lukens?

One, I suppose, minor revelation served to bring Folwell and me closer together. My gun wasn't the murder weapon. It was a larger caliber, no markings that appeared on the slugs that had been pried out of the brains of X and Lukens.

"When do I get it back?" I asked Folwell. We were alone together in Dick Carson's private office. We had been waiting there for the phone call that never came from the "kidnapper."

"Someone will bring it back from the barracks when they're coming this way," Folwell said. He was fishing in a deep sea, just as I was, for answers. He had decided to focus his attention on the missing Chips. Chips hadn't shown. It had been at least six hours now since he'd left his uneaten breakfast on the serving table in the kitchen. He had vanished into nowhere.

"From what the old lady told you, Chips was very close to Wilfred Krider," Folwell said.

"At least very grateful to him," I said.

"Krider was using this damn tape to hold over Lukens' head, according to the wife," Folwell said. "He didn't give it to you or Miss Walton to keep for him. Chips and Dick Carson, who were also close to Krider and owed him—for this inn,—are the next best bets. Krider must have trusted them both."

"So Chips kills two men who are trying to find the tape and runs out in the middle of his breakfast? Running points right at him, doesn't it? But if I had done it I wouldn't run for that very reason. Dick Carson hasn't run anywhere."

"Damn!" Folwell said.

"And while you're aiming at Chips," I said, "there are a couple of other things that bother me."

"Only a couple?"

"Either Chips or Carson could easily have hidden X's body around this dump for a couple of days. They knew every inch of the place.

"So does Fritz Schlee, the chef, and Grover Jones and Tom Bentley, the outdoor men, and Mildred the maid, and who else," I said. "As a matter of fact, anyone who read Millicent Hawthorne's book on the inn. That book took Lukens to that walled-in staircase."

"So what bothers you?" Folwell asked.

"If Chips was hanging onto that tape for Krider or Carson, why rip up Teddy?"

"Teddy?"

"The Duchess's teddy bear," I said. "That toy bear was stolen, ripped open, all the stuffing torn out. Why? Somebody was looking for something—something that would fit into a coffee cup or the toe of a shoe. The tape. If Chips or Carson had the tape they wouldn't go looking for it in the Duchess's good luck toy."

Folwell nodded slowly. "I've thought of that," he said. "Things were pretty scattered around here when the Duchess sounded the alarm about a body in the pool. Troopers coming and going, people coming and going. Miss Walton was brought down to the bar for questioning. She didn't bring the bear, remember? She said he didn't like strangers." He swore, softly. "Lukens could have slipped up that walled-in staircase in the confusion to look for his precious tape. He hears somebody coming, grabs up the bear, and retreats the way he came. He cuts open the bear and looks for his tape. It isn't there. Early this morning he goes back for another search and somebody plugs him."

"I've got a nice little road block for you there," I said. "Lukens didn't buy that book in the gift shop until the morning *after* X was found in the pool. You saying he knew about the staircase before he bought the book?"

"Anything could be," Folwell said. "Damn, damn, damn!"

"I've been playing games, too," I said. "As you say, anything could be. For size, try this. Krider has something on Lukens preserved on a tape. Lukens hired X to come to Camden to find it. He blows it—I blow it by shooting at him. Someone helps X get away. It's too risky to try it again. Krider is alive and on guard. Then the Old Man dies, suddenly and unexpectedly. They wait in fear for the tape to be revealed by whomever Krider gave it to. Nothing happens; it doesn't appear in his belongings, nor is it mentioned in his will, or in the long time it takes to settle his Estate. Now Lukens' big moment is at hand. He's about to become top dog in Krider Industries, something the Old Man didn't want to happen. Krider long dead, could have arranged to destroy Lukens when that moment came. Whoever has the tape has instructions. Lukens has to take one more shot at finding it."

"The instructions were to murder anyone who comes looking for the tape?" Folwell said. "Come on, Dan!" You commit murder out of loyalty to a dead man?"

"Maybe. Like you said, could be. But come with me a little farther. Lukens hired X to come back to Camden. X knows the layout here. He's supposed to report back to Lukens. He doesn't. He was killed on Monday sometime, his body hidden. On Tuesday, back in Summit, Lukens knows something has gone wrong. He advances his vacation by two or three days and he and his wife drive up here, registering under her brother's name. No sign of X. Then, on their first night here, X turns up in the pool! To Lukens that means that the person who has the tape is here, that X knew who it was and got himself bumped off. He has to pull off the job himself now. The guy with the tape is waiting for him."

"Chips or Carson," Folwell said.

"We've got a Mr. X," I said. "It could be a Mr. Y or a Mr. Z."

"So you wind up nowhere," Folwell said.

"I wish Mark Stone would call back," I said. "He could know what Krider had on Lukens. Whatever it was it doesn't matter now to Krider Industries. Lukens is dead."

I tried that number again I had for Stone. The polite secretary told me she hadn't been in touch with Stone since my earlier calls. But he must know, she assured me, about Lukens. It was all over the TV screens and on the radio.

The day wore on, the kind of day you don't want to remember. Troopers were all over the inn and the town. Among other things they were looking for Chips, who had turned away from his perfectly cooked breakfast and disappeared. Folwell, who could only play his own hunches, had had Dick Carson on the carpet for hours, it seemed. Without any positive result.

I roamed the inn, the grounds, not knowing what I was looking for. A strange face that would ring some kind of bell out of the past? I reported to the Duchess from time to time. The young trooper, Chapman, had been ordered to give the old lady as much privacy as possible. He was camped out in the hallway outside her rooms. He seemed very content with a copy of *Playboy*. I noticed he marked the center-fold with his thumb each time I passed him. The Duchess had had no callers, he told me.

The Duchess seemed to relax after I told her Mrs. Lukens' account of the kidnapping.

"It's a relief to know that Laura's worrying about her musical comedy and not her life, Daniel."

"Did Wilfred never talk to you about Kenneth Lukens?" I asked her. "He seems to have had something on Lukens, and yet Lukens stayed on at Krider Industries."

"Back at that time—when you drove off Mr. X—he talked a lot about 'the disease of power,'" the Duchess said. "He said there were men in high places in the corporation who might want to see him dead. He never mentioned any specific names."

"And you didn't ask him?"

"It was understood that I wouldn't ask him questions about the business."

We kicked it back and forth and got no place. She'd known there was such a person as Kenneth Lukens, but not from the Old Man. Lukens' name appeared in press releases about Krider Industries, and she had them all in her stacks of old newspapers. But it had just been a name, along with a dozen others.

"The other day you warned me not to trust Mark Stone," I said. "Why?"

She was silent for a moment. "That time ten years ago—Will thought your Mr. X couldn't have got past the gate, past the electric fence, and to the house unless Stone's men, the guards, had been told to look the other way. The security was too tight, too perfect, Will thought. I don't think he fully trusted Stone after that. I know he suggested it to you. He told me he had. I was just reminding you, Daniel."

It was true. Krider had wondered about Stone. I was wondering about him, too, as the day proceeded into twilight. The polite secretary had gotten a little impatient with me as I began calling every hour. Lukens' death had to be a matter of concern to Krider Industries. Why hadn't Stone called? Why wasn't he here?

And then, just at dusk, I thought I saw him. I was standing at the windows in the Duchess's jumble room on one of my checkouts with her. She, apparently worn out by the last twenty-four hours, was resting in her bedroom. The jumble room windows overlook the pool. In the last vestige of daylight, a tall, lean figure came around the corner of the building and stood looking down into the water. The light was too dim to be sure, but I could have sworn it was Stone. I leaned out the window.

"Stone!" I shouted.

The man didn't move. He just stood staring into the water.

"Stone!" I shouted again.

He never looked my way, but turned and walked slowly around the corner of the building again.

It might be, it might not be. I had to be sure.

I charged out into the hall, almost catching Chapman with his center-fold spread out for total viewing.

"Get word to Folwell if you can," I said to him. "Tell him I think I just saw Mark Stone out by the pool."

With his thumb carefully marking the key page, Chapman stood up. "There's a phone in the linen room down the hall. If it's important—."

"It's important, and I can't stop to do it," I said.

Folwell had been right about one thing. Murder wasn't doing Dick Carson's business any harm. The lobby area outside the dining room was already crowding with people who had just "dropped in" for dinner or supper and found they should have reserved. Voices from the lounge were cheery. I knew a lot of these people, locals, and they all had questions for me.

"Sorry. Get back to you," I kept repeating, as I did my best imitation of running an off-tackle slant without any interferers in front of me.

Lights from the main building reflected in the pool. No

swimmers tonight. I sprinted around the corner of the inn to the parking lot. It was jammed. Unless my man had been parked right at the entrance I didn't think he could have beaten me out of the lot.

Some wit once wrote a line about his hero "riding off in all directions at once." I ran in and out of the lanes of parked cars, looking for one which had a driver in it. If the man I'd seen was Stone he'd had iron nerves not to react to my shouting his name. Stone, from what I knew of him, was that well-trained.

There was a short, squat black man wearing a chauffeur's cap sitting in a Cadillac. He hadn't noticed anyone in a hurry—a man wearing a dark business suit.

I headed for the outside door that opens onto a narrow stair leading down to the catacombs. The kitchen area was humming; well-organized confusion. Fritz Schlee spotted me and gave me his frozen smile. He gave his tall chef's hat a little tug downward.

"You want to live down here I can rent you a nice freezer compartment," he said.

"You remember a man named Stone, security chief for Krider Industries, who was around here ten years ago? Tall, slim, rock-faced guy?"

"He's supposed to be down here? Nobody who isn't supposed to be down here at the dinner hour is down here," Fritz said. "That goes for you, too, Burton. Out!"

Someone who didn't belong in the kitchen would stand out like a sore thumb. Damn Stone if he'd come here without letting me know. I stopped by Dominic's short-order griddle.

"You still looking for Chips?" Dominic asked.

I told him who I was looking for. He shrugged. "No strangers been down here in the last hour when I came on," he said. "Hamburger, rare with no lettuce." He slid a plate along the counter to a waitress.

I climbed the stairs back up to the parking lot. I hadn't called Stone's number for about an hour. He might have gotten in touch in that hour, told his girl he was here. My cottage just across the street was the quietest place at this time to try calling again.

I went in the kitchen way, switched on lights, and headed for the phone in the study. The polite secretary answered promptly.

"I'm sorry. I haven't heard from Mr. Stone since you first called this morning," she said.

"I think I just saw him up here at the Red Cardinal Inn."

"Then you know more about him than I do, Mr. Burton."

"Is it like him to stay out-of-touch for a whole day?"

"I've known him to be out-of-touch for a month when he's on a job," the girl said.

I put down the phone and reached for a cigarette in the box on the desk.

"When you don't want anyone to know where you are you stay out-of-touch," a smooth voice said from behind me.

I spun around in my chair and found myself facing Mark Stone. He stood in the doorway, pointing a gun right at my chest. I squeezed my left arm against my body and realized those bastards hadn't brought my gun back from the ballistics barrel in the barracks.

"It's about time you showed up," I said, as though I didn't see his gun.

"I wanted to meet you on my terms," he said. "Two murders is enough."

"What the hell are you talking about?"

"Open up your coat," he said. "Carefully."

"If you're looking for my gun, I don't have it," I said. I opened my jacket to reveal my empty holster. "It's at the trooper barracks where they tested it out. It wasn't the gun that killed Mr. X and Lukens, if that's what interests you."

"A guy like you can carry extra heat," he said. "Stand up and turn around."

I've been frisked before. This man was an expert. He went over me from the back of my neck to my ankles.

"Turn around and sit down," he said. "Keep your hands

on the desk." I obeyed orders. "Now we can talk."

"I've been trying to get to talk to you all day," I said. "It *is* a tape Lukens and X were after, right?"

"Why ask me?" he said. "I told you that much this morning, didn't I?"

"I've wondered why you told me."

"Because I want it," Stone said. The gun in his hand was frighteningly steady.

"I haven't got it," I said. "Miss Walton hasn't got it. I haven't got the faintest damned idea who *has* got it."

"There are two ways out of this for you," Stone said. "If your price isn't too high I'll pay it. If you keep trying to play games with me I'll leave you with your brains spilled out on the top of that desk."

"I'm not playing games. I don't have the tape. I don't know who has."

I saw he didn't believe me.

Then I nearly fell out of my chair. Just behind him a tall figure loomed. The Duchess, dressed for dinner, decked out in her jewels, was not a foot away from him. I opened my mouth to shout at her. Stone saw me reacting to something and started to turn.

The old lady had more than diamond rings on her hands. She was holding a small, pearl-handled revolver. She fired it right at his left temple and he pitched, face down, on the rug.

"I think, Daniel," she said, her voice quite steady, "I'd appreciate a glass of water."

You do crazy things at a moment like that. Would you believe I stepped over Stone's body—I knew he was dead—went to the kitchen, and got the Duchess a glass of water?

I brought it back, and she turned away and took a couple of swallows. She put the glass down on my desk.

"I don't know how long it will take," she said, "but I think I'd appreciate it if you'd walk me back to my rooms. I'd like it to happen there."

"Like what to happen?" And I think I knew before she

told me.

"A long time ago Will Krider gave me a tablet to take in case somebody tried to force me to talk about him. I've just taken it, Daniel. I think it must be reasonably quick."

Her long, slender fingers fastened around my wrist were unbelievable strong. We walked slowly across the highway, across the lawns, to the Red Cardinal. She was leaning more heavily on me than I could remember her doing before.

"I now what you're thinking, Daniel," she said. She sounded, for Pete's sake, like a fond parent. "You're thinking of trying to call a doctor to stop this. You're thinking of inviting Lieutenant Folwell to hear my confession." Folwell was never going to get his promotion to captain from her. "Stone was going to kill you, you know."

"I know, luv. I was about to say my beads when I saw you!"

"I saw him go to your house from my windows," she said. "You shouted to him, and while you were running downstairs I saw him cross the highway. What is it they call it in the movies? I knew you were headed for a—a 'shoot-out.' So, please, just take me to my rooms, and let me tell you how it was. There may not be time for Lieutenant Folwell to ask me for my name and address again, or for a doctor to mess around with trying to save a life that no longer needs saving."

We walked through the crowded lobby and up the stairs to the second floor. As she opened the door to her jumble room I was aware of an unfamiliar, acrid odor.

"Something burning," I said.

She smiled at me, an almost tender smile. "The tape," she said. "I left it burning in the basin in my bathroom."

"You've had the tape all this time?"

She nodded.

"My God, what a magnificent liar you are!?" I said.

"Women learn the art very early in life," she said. "Please, Daniel, I think I'd like to lie down on my bed. I shouldn't like to find myself stumbling around suddenly, or falling."

"I'm not doing the right thing, you know," I said. "I should be getting help."

"To keep me alive? No point, Daniel, no point at all. I've done the last thing I could on earth for Will Krider. I'm really quite ready to go, my friend."

I walked her to the bedroom. She paused in the doorway, smiling faintly at the painting of her magnificent nudity fifty years ago. Then she lay down on the bed, her eyes closed for a minute. I was afraid she was going to slip away before she could tell me anything. I covered her with a light-weight summer quilt that was folded on the foot of the bed.

"Teddy was not just a good luck gift," she said. "Will was always concerned with protecting me from his kind of violent world. Teddy was good luck because inside him was my little gun. I was a walking 'gun moll' all those years. And for the last ten years that famous tape has been inside Teddy, ready to be used if it had to be."

"I don't understand. I've never understood . . . ?"

Her eyelids fluttered and she raised a hand to silence me. "Please, Daniel, let me tell it. Because I . . . I don't think there is very much time."

"Are you hurting? Are you in pain?"

"Please, Daniel!" It seemed to me she was finding it hard to breathe. "I can't tell you too much about the tape, though I've played it many times. Fifteen years ago, in the Middle East, the Shah of Zadir was assassinated. There followed a massacre of about ten thousand people in that country. You may remember. Krider Industries was behind the assassination. It was a plan of Kenneth Lukens', based on faulty information provided by Mark Stone's security people, approved by Will Krider. If the truth ever leaked out Krider Industries would have been seriously damaged. Like so many other transactions of Will's, the whole scheme, a conference between Will and Lukens and Stone, was taped. Will kept it, though it would have been safer for everyone if he'd destroyed it. But he kept it and later he was glad. He and Lukens became enemies inside the company. Lukens saw himself as Will's successor. Will saw him as an incompetent who had bungled the business in Zadir. The tape, made public, would end Lukens' career at Krider, and, incidentally, Mark Stone's.

"Ten years ago, Lukens and Stone decided to send someone here to find that tape. You call him Mr. X. Last Monday, he told me his name. It was Something Clinton, or Clinton Somebody. He asked me for the tape. He knew somehow that I kept it in Teddy. I don't know how he knew, maybe it was just a good guess. I walked into the jumble room, carrying Teddy. We'd been for our morning walk. Clinton demanded Teddy and the tape.

"I pretended to open up Teddy to get the tape, took out my gun, and shot him."

"My God!" I said. "But the body was hidden for two days. How—?"

"Please, Daniel, let me finish. Where better to hide a body but in my jumble room, under those stacks of papers. Nobody dared touch them or move them. But I—I was afraid he would become—noticeable. I spent two days trying to think out what to do. I—I tried moving the body, but I simply didn't have the strength."

"I should think not. So how—?"

She gave me a very faint smile. "Have you ever wondered, Daniel, if you had let me down, or Dick Carson had let me down?"

"The Old Man would have dropped a thunderbolt on us," I suggested.

"Chips," she said. "Dear Chips. He has two great loyalties: to Will Krider and to this inn. If you or Dick Carson had run out on me, Chips would have reported to Wilfred's lawyer who controls his estate."

"The Old Man left nothing to chance," I said.

"Never. Well, I had to have help, so I sent for Chips."

"He got rid of the body for you?"

She nodded. "Out the window and into the pool. He felt Will would have wanted him to help me." She drew a deep, shuddering breath.

"Then, yesterday I was in the next room. I heard sounds in here. I was just in time to see my dressing table pushed aside and Lukens climbing in the old window. I was ready this time."

"But Teddy was gone, stolen, ripped open."

"I did that, Daniel. If Clinton knew I'd carried the tape in Teddy he might have told someone else. When Teddy was found destroyed, that someone else would think someone had beaten him to the tape, stolen it from me. Lukens just had time to tell me he knew Teddy's destruction must have been a fake. I was carrying my gun in my dress pocket and I shot him. He tumbled back through the window and down the old walled-in staircase."

"Chips?" I said.

"Dear Chips," she said. "He was getting his breakfast in the catacombs when he saw Lukens slip down the tunnel there and head for the old staircase. We were all suddenly together in the darkness—Chips, and the dead Lukens, and me."

"Where is Chips?"

"He's all right, Daniel. I would never let him be involved, you understand. I persuaded him to go to Washington to talk to Will Krider's lawyers. I knew that sooner or later I might need that kind of help."

"But all you had to do was turn over the tape to the authorities, and Lukens and Stone would have been properly punished!"

"I promised Will I'd do just that," she said. "He said it wouldn't matter after he was gone. But—but I played the tape over and over, Daniel. It revealed Will as a villain, too. He would suddenly be remembered as the mastermind behind the massacre of thousands of people. I—I couldn't let that happen to his memory, Daniel. I loved him—so very much. Please, Daniel," she whispered. "Keep my secret."

She made a choking sound. She had spoken her own epitaph.

I loved him—so very much.

I stood there for a long time looking at her. Then I reached up and took the nude painting down from the wall. The gawking young Chapman, the other troopers, the local press, were not entitled to invade that privacy, I decided.

The Berkshire Traveller Press publishes books on travel, history, country living, Shaker customs and furniture, and cookbooks, as well as works of fiction: adult, juvenile, and historical.

Authors' inquiries are invited. Please send a two to four-page outline of the work with a self-addressed, stamped return envelope. Unsolicited manuscripts are not accepted.